Murder on Had
A Romano-British M
A novel by Andrew

Text Copyright (c) 2013 Andrew Drummond
All Rights Reserved

Dedication:

To the memory of Kitty Drummond; good friend, companion and cat without equal.

Picture Acknowledgement:

The Cover Photograph was taken by *clarita* and can be found at *morguefiles.com*

Preface

Rome was the greatest empire that the world had ever seen. It eclipsed everything that had gone before it and most that came after it. From the founding of the city in BC 753 and the subsequent eclipse of Etruscan power in ancient Italy, Rome went from strength to strength. There had been the occasional wobble; in BC 390 the Celts had humbled and sacked an ill prepared city and army. But after military reforms had been made and implemented, the Roman army created the empire. It carried the city to one successful conquest after another. Eventually, the whole of the known world was subservient to, and paid homage to, the eternal city. But like all of the world's great empires, it reached and passed its zenith. By 350 AD, the Roman rule of her vast territories was already in terminal decline. The great power was creaking at the seams and in the process of dividing itself into two. Constantine I had moved the capital of the empire east, in 330 AD, to the city that we now call Istanbul. Constantius I had divided Britain itself into four provinces, some thirty years earlier. In 350 AD, an usurper of German descent, called Magnentius, had seized the western throne. In the process he had killed his rival, the legitimate emperor and son of Constantine, Constans I. Throughout the empire, citizens and soldiers awaited developments and feared for the future.

Britannia, the northernmost boundary of the imperial power, reacted like most other provinces. Individuals still carried on with their daily lives and duties, but they lived in an atmosphere of uncertainty and worry. Across the length and breadth of England, from Dover in the south, to Hadrian's Wall in the North, the country was populated by well over a thousand settlements that regarded themselves as Roman. Since the successful invasion of the country by the emperor Claudius in 43 AD, after Julius Caesar's abortive attempt in BC 55, Britannia had gradually become Romanised. This was not withstanding the subsequent rebellions of Caractacus, in 59 AD and that of Boudicea, in 60 AD, both of which were ruthlessly suppressed by the occupying power. But rebellious Britain was treated no differently to any other troublesome province. Roman rule was built on the concept of obedience from its subservient territories. Any deviation would be punished, and was punished very harshly, until order had been restored and guaranteed.

Over the next three hundred years of occupation, our ancestors, like many peoples across Europe, realised the benefits of belonging to Rome. They took up citizenship and turning away from rebellion, embraced their conqueror's way of life. Eventually Britain became a fully integrated part of the empire. The protection of the standing army enforced peace on tribes that had previously been constantly at war with each other. But it is a tribute to our forefathers' bellicose nature, that three Roman legions were permanently stationed on a small island. But the Pax Romana was only one aspect of Roman life in Britain. Contact with the continent brought trade and the import of luxury goods from the Mediterranean. There were also the codes and justice of Roman law, many of which survive to this day, to ensure fairness in citizens' dealings with each other. Under Roman rule life was probably better for the ordinary person than it had been in the latter part of the Iron Age.

But that was about to change and it is this background against which this novel is set. It explores the problems that most typical Romano-British citizens faced, as the world's greatest ever imperial power, slowly crumbled in the west and abandoned them to their fate. And it was a grim fate too - when the last vestiges of Roman power vanished, around 410 AD, England soon entered what historians call the dark ages. These lasted for almost five hundred years, as the country faced both the Saxon and later the Viking invasions, prior to the Norman Conquest in the eleventh century. During those years, civilisation declined to the point of vanishing and life became short and brutal. Other than surviving monastic texts, which are few in number, there is little written evidence of this period of history.

    The majority of this story takes place in the imaginary community of Virulanium, a fort and settlement, located towards the eastern side of Hadrian's Wall. There were 17 such forts, spread along the seventy-three mile length of the Wall, one every seven miles. The Romans calculated the Wall to be eighty miles long, as their miles were slightly shorter than the measurement that we use today. Birdoswald, Chesters and Wallsend are three of the real life historic northern wall forts and settlements, which are still being excavated by archaeologists and yielding fascinating finds to this day. One prominent and respected archaeologist estimates that only five percent of the Wall has been properly excavated. He also expects exciting developments to take place over the next two hundred years, once funding becomes available. The results of his work can be seen at Vindolanda, a fort and settlement one mile to the south of Hadrian's Wall, some 13 miles from Hexham. Vindolanda pre dates the wall and was part of an earlier defensive line called the Stanegate frontier.

    In 350 AD Virulanium would have been, like many Roman communities, a long established site.

Outside the fort there would have been a settlement, or *vicus*, which relied on the military for its living. This would have grown from being a originally collection of camp followers, to a fully-fledged community. There would also have been a variety of houses, shops, craftsmen and other public amenities. Many of the inhabitants would be retired army veterans and their children grew up to provide the next generation of soldiers. As such, they would have been following in the footsteps of their fathers, who had followed the exact same route themselves. In the latter days of the Roman Empire only five percent of serving legionnaires were from the Italian peninsular.

    The construction of a twelve-foot high wall had begun following the Emperor Hadrian's visit to Britain in 122 AD. This was just one stop on his audit of the entire Roman Empire. The first version of the structure took only six years for the legions to build. In the east, the Wall was conceived and built as a stone fortification, which ran westwards to the river Irthing. But from Bowness, in the west, the fortification was originally built as a series of earth ramparts and ditches. This was the traditional Roman way of building such a barrier and ran east to the river Irthing. However, the western turf ramparts were soon replaced with stone. We cannot be sure when this was done, but most historians believe it was completed by 150 AD, if not earlier. In a sense, the Wall was never actually finished, as construction and modification continued throughout the Roman occupation of Britain.

    As to why the Wall was built, historians originally thought that it was due to the activities of the Picts or Scots. But more recent assessments believe that the Picts arrived in Scotland after the wall was built. They are not recorded in written history until 297 AD, when they were described as aggressive, northern enemies of Rome. Just to confuse matters, the Scots did not colonise Scotland until the 5th Century AD and they originated from Ireland! Although there can be no doubt that barbarian transgressions across the border long pre date recorded history. The emperor Hadrian's biographer stated that the wall was built to "separate Romans from the barbarians". The modern consensus is that the Wall was constructed to state the northern boundary of the empire. Hadrian, having taken stock of the size of his vast empire, decreed that there would be no further expansion in any direction. As far as Britain was concerned, this meant no further northern conquests. The Wall was constructed and became an obstacle to the barbarians, rather than an impenetrable barrier. But generations of men, women and children lived in the shadow of their raids. They also lived behind the Wall, from what is now Wallsend in the east, to modern day Bowness in the west. For the most part, they served the empire loyally and that loyalty was rewarded, with the benefits of citizenship. However, by 350 AD events in Virulanium and England were starting to take a dramatic turn, both locally and within the context of the break up of the empire.

Timeline and note about the glossary:

To set the events in their proper historical context and give a guide to the chronology, here is a list of the Roman emperors mentioned in the novel and their reigns;

Tiberius: 14 to 37 AD
Caligula: 37 to 41 AD
Claudius: 41 to 54 AD
Hadrian: 117 to 138 AD
Constantius I: 293 to 306 AD
Constantine I: 312 to 337 AD
Constantine II: 337 to 340 AD
Constans I: 337 to 350 AD
Constantanius II: 337 to 361 AD (Ruler of the eastern empire only)
Magnentius: 350 to 353 AD (The German Usurper)

337 AD was also the year of three emperors, all of whom were brothers and sons of Constantine I. Julius Caesar is not included in the list because he was never an emperor and Rome was still a republic in his lifetime. But amongst the many official titles that he held was dictator for life. He was assassinated in BC 44.

In the interests of historical accuracy, I have tried to use original Roman place names and terms, where appropriate. These are set out in *italics*, alongside their modern translation, at the end of the novel. They are also shown in *italics*, on the first occasion that they are used in the body of the text.

Chapter One

It was very late when Versillius, the centurion, left Caracalla's tavern. He had spent the whole evening in there, with several of his men, drinking far too much cloudy beer than was good for him. Not that the alcohol that was a problem for the centurion to handle, at least in his opinion. But the murky taste of the opaque beverage was another matter entirely. Nobody drank the settlement's locally brewed beer out of choice. It was consumed out of necessity. This was because in these days of shortages, there was precious little wine to be found so far north. So the locally brewed ale was all that there was available for legionnaires or ordinary citizens to drink. He had promised the soldiers an evening out, at his expense, because they had spent a week repairing the crumbling masonry of the Wall. As they had also caught and executed two Picts, he was of the opinion that they deserved a treat.

After all, he could still just about afford it. Centurions were paid better wages than ordinary soldiers, twenty times as much in fact. This reflected their seniority, experience and greater value to the empire. Although, the physical payment of money was dependent upon coffers, from the continent, actually arriving in the settlement. This did not happen so regularly in these times of change and upheaval in the western empire. In the absence of new coins from abroad, soldiers were paid directly from the fort's treasury. Unfortunately that was at a reduced rate. The civic clerks maintained a ledger of the differences, which were made good if and when a new shipment was finally delivered.

Versillius was a short, stocky man of around five foot four inches in height. He possessed a broad girth, especially around his shoulders. Out of uniform, he had often been mistaken for a blacksmith, rather than a soldier. He was forty-five years of age and the first traces of grey were starting to show in his reddish, brown hair. The centurion's years of service in the Roman army had been kind to him, as he had the physique and fitness level of a man ten years his junior. Maybe his stomach muscles were not as tight as they used to be. He put this down to his repeated visits to the settlement's bar and other less salubrious premises. Caracalla's tavern was located in the eastern *vicus*, on the southern side of the fort of Virulanium, just outside the building's strong walls. Rather than returning directly to the barracks, Versillius decided to take a circular route and breathe in some of the cool night air. As his head began to clear, the centurion walked through the empty piazza and crossed the via south. This took him past the fountain and temple of Jupiter and then through the deserted western forum and market place. Versillius was glad to see that the street torches were lit. He was feeling just a little bit drunk and needed the light to help him make his way back to the barracks without falling over. In an attempt to sober up, he sat by the fountain for several minutes and listened to the sound of the water splashing into the basin. Above him, the night sky was, as always, cloudy and promised rain. If not now, then in the morning, for sure – he told himself. Even in this month of Julius the British weather was still cold and wet.

    The centurion had stayed on in the tavern later than his men, but had decided against visiting the house of pleasure. His detail needed to rise early on the following day, to continue their work repairing the

Wall. Besides, he had drunk too much ale to perform well with the prostitutes, a problem which was manifesting itself too frequently for his liking. Other than fighting the *barbarians* and patching up the Wall, the life of a single soldier at the northern extremity of the western empire, was quite limited. Off duty activities comprised of playing games such as dice or drinking and whoring. Any of which came as a source of great relief from repair work. As the great structure was now over two hundred years old, it was in constant need of maintenance. The work was hard, involving the making of mortar and carrying back breaking, heavy stones from the quarries. It also required constant vigilance, because of the threat posed by Pictish raiding parties. Whatever privations were now suffered on this side of the border, the Romans still had much more cattle, food and possessions than their northern neighbours. Hence, the constant threat to Virulanium and the other settlements in the surrounding area, of coming under attack from the barbarians.

Putting these thoughts to one side, he rose to his feet and resumed his journey through the forum, sidestepping the rubbish left by the market traders. Leaving the fountain behind, he walked past the temple and towards the fort's southern gate. Just inside the fort, were the offices of the administration, where the prefect and governor spent most of their time, closeted with their officials. He made a mental note to address them on the subject of the vendors' rubbish. Their lack of tidiness was getting worse by the day, and sober or not, any citizen could easily be tripped over by their refuse. Of course, it would be easier for him to talk to the prefect, Gaius Flavius. As the settlement's only centurion, Versillius reported directly to the town's most senior, civic official. That was because his legion's *legate*, or general, was based over a hundred miles away to the south west, in another fort called *Deva*. In keeping with the commanding officer's character, it was well away from any danger posed not only by the Picts, but any other potential enemy. Versillius tried to recall which writer or philosopher had originally commented on the privileges offered by rank and high office.

He was still pondering the question, when he left the forum and approached the cobbled street that would take him back to the barracks. Even though the torchlight was now some distance behind the centurion, he could just about make out a prostrate form lying face down, at the side of the short, but wide road. Thinking that it was one of his men, who had collapsed in an alcohol, induced stupor on the way home, he bent over and shook the man.

"Wake up you fool!" he said, "There's work for you to do when the sunrises. This is the last time that I take you out to get drunk."

There was no reply and as his eyes had now adjusted to the darkness, he was able to see that it was not one of his soldiers. Although his cloak and garb were that of a Roman citizen, the man's cloak was a *pallium*. This was the large, rectangular outer garment worn by civilians. Similarly, his *tunica* was not military in style, as the hem was worn low beneath his knees, almost to the ankles. Versillius rolled the man over, now concerned for the person's safety and puzzled as to his identity. His fears seemed justified, because despite being manhandled, there was still no sound or response from him. The centurion quickly realised this was due to the fact that he was dead, when he saw the man's open, lifeless eyes, after he had turned him over. Despite the dark night, he could make out the auburn hair and bearded features of

Antonius, chief scribe to the prefect and governor. Versillius pulled the pallium open and could see and feel traces of wet blood on the front of the scribe's toga. Touching the man's forehead, he found that the body was still warm, so realised that Antonius could not have been dead for long.

Then thinking that the scribe's assailant might still be in the vicinity, he held his breath and glanced around anxiously. But in the surrounding darkness, he could see nobody and heard no sounds, other than the splashing of Virulanium's fountain. Relieved that he was alone, albeit with a dead man, Versillius decided to summon help. Using his loudest parade ground voice, he yelled, in the direction of the southern gate, "Night watch, members of the night watch, your centurion summons you. I order you to come quickly, a man has been murdered!"

He only had to shout the words one more time, before he was swiftly approached by five legionnaires from the barracks, carrying weapons and torches. The night watch had answered his summons promptly and swiftly. The leader of the watch was Marcus, one of his better soldiers. Unlike his comrades and centurion, he didn't gamble or grumble about his lot in life. He also spent very little time in the tavern or the house of pleasure, being dedicated to progressing his career in the army. Marcus was a tall, dark haired man, of almost six feet and just under twenty-six years of age. Standing to attention before Versillius, he said, "One of the men heard your voice, from the southern tower, sir, where he was standing guard for the night. I organised this patrol and we came to you as quickly as was possible."

As he spoke, the other men in the detail glanced down at the corpse. "At least it is not one of ours," one soldier, Trajanius, muttered audibly to his comrades, "It looks like that stupid, old fool of a chief scribe..."

Instantly, Marcus turned to him, saying, "Legionnaire, you are on duty and in the presence of our commanding officer. Neither the centurion, nor I, asked for your opinion. If I hear one more word from you then you will feel the force of your comrades' rods. Do you understand me?"

The leader of the watch was referring to the punishment meted out by fellow soldiers to transgressors of the Roman army's strict code of military discipline. Trajanius, a skinny, balding man, in his mid thirties, bowed his head in acknowledgement of the rebuke and grumbled an apology. Both Marcus and the centurion realised that the apology was made with only a half hearted and grudging tone in the man's voice. But Versillius was quite impressed with the attitude of the young watch commander. Long before he had taken to the tavern and the house of pleasure, he had been as strict with the men under his command, while he rose through the ranks. Although as his time in the army had passed, he had relaxed his approach to discipline – both professional and personal. Recognising that the five soldiers were now awaiting his instructions, the centurion said, "Marcus, have the rest of your patrol take the scribe's corpse back to the barracks. It will be examined after we have spoken to the prefect and roused Artemis, the physician. As you all know, Antonius was our administration's chief, civic servant. Like myself, he reported directly to the prefect. Therefore, I must inform Gaius Flavius immediately. And you, Marcus, will accompany me, as you are the commander of the watch. I have no doubt that the prefect will want to hear your version of events. But first tell me, have there been any signs of infiltration by our northern neighbours tonight?"

"No, sir," the young watch commander responded, "As always, I ensured that we kept a vigilant look out, throughout the duty. But neither I or the men, saw or heard anything from the other side of the Wall."

The four legionnaires nodded swiftly in agreement with his words. The young man's explanation sounded quite plausible to Versillius. But his years of experience caused him to mistrust not Marcus, but the detail. They had agreed with their commander too quickly and too readily. The centurion addressed the four soldiers directly, "Nobody caught even the faintest sniff, of a Pictish raiding party, on the night air?"

They all shook their heads from side to side, as Trajanius chanced his arm again, by saying, "The only smell that I detected was the beer from Caracalla's tavern. I dare say, that you know more about that smell than we do, sir!"

The other three men sniggered at his comments. Versillius was about to respond, when Marcus said, "Trajanius, that will certainly do. I do not want to have to reprimand you again! Now, centurion, I can assure you that until we heard your summons, the night had passed quietly and without any incident whatsoever."

The scribe's murder placed Versillius in a difficult position. As the town's only centurion he was also responsible for its law and order, under the orders of the prefect. Even if their northern neighbours had killed the man, it would be his responsibility to find and punish the killer. But as the fort's watch had detected no incursions that night, then he could only assume that whoever had committed the crime lived in, or close to Virulanium – on the southern side of the great wall. And that meant mounting an investigation within the local community. The centurion watched as the four soldiers of the detail picked up the scribe's dead body, without any great enthusiasm. As they carried it off, in the direction of the barracks, Versillius was annoyed to see that they were virtually dragging the corpse along the stones of the cobbled street. "Be careful how you do that," he shouted at them, "I do not want to lose any more evidence or for the dead man's skin to get any further cuts and bruises!"

At his words, the men suddenly gripped the dead man's arms and feet tightly, standing more upright as they walked. Satisfied, that his admonishment had increased their interest in the task, he then set off towards the western side of the vicus. This was one of the two parts of the civilian settlement, which were situated outside of the fort. It was also the place where the prefect lived, in his palatial villa. Marcus followed him, apprehensively, wanting to talk. But the younger man was unsure, as to whether or not to address his superior officer, before being spoken to himself. Rank and precedence played an important part in maintaining the discipline of the Roman army.

As they walked through the western vicus, towards the high status villas, the centurion felt pleased that he had Marcus to accompany him. He had personally trained the younger man, from when he had joined the army. That was as a young recruit, some five years previously. Since then he had kept a watchful eye over his rapid progress through the ranks. This was partly due to the fact that Versillius had served alongside Marcus' father, for many years. Unfortunately, he had died, when Marcus was still a child, shortly after taking his pension. Although they had been friends, he had never been able to completely understand the young man's father. For instance, he had adopted the *patrician* Roman *praenomen* of Marcus, even though he was of humble Spanish descent. This had been a cause of great amusement to the rest of the garrison and remained such to this day. It was why Marcus was known as Marcus, rather than by his *cognomen* of Pontius. And then, there had also been the father's involvement in the cult of Mithras, at a time when the strange, eastern religion was on the verge of being proscribed. Despite several warnings from Versillius, he had refused to listen and his career had suffered as a result. But at least the centurion had seen the son grow up free of the father's stubborn, awkward nature and irritating religious beliefs.

Chapter Two

Versillius had recently purchased a villa in the eastern vicus, pending his imminent retirement. He had almost completed his twenty-five years in the army, having started as a twenty-year old raw recruit, during the reign of Constantine the first. On completion of such a length of service, an ordinary soldier from the ranks, was usually pensioned off. A single legionnaire would then normally take a wife. Nowadays, it was more likely that he would marry the local woman, who was the mother of his children. Then the man would live out his days in the area surrounding the fort, becoming a member of the community that he had served. As a centurion, Versillius had the option of serving beyond his term. This was because the legion found it hard to replace the experience and knowledge of its senior non commissioned officers. But the centurion had seen enough of military life, especially in these days of uncertainty and he now looked forward to leaving the army.

Although the soldiers and citizens of the settlement were called Roman, virtually all of the inhabitants of Virulanium had never been further south than a few miles away from the Wall. He, himself had only visited Deva, the twentieth legion's home base, on a few occasions. Versillius recognised the facts and though he had heard wonderful stories about life in the Mediterranean world, he knew inside himself that he would never see or experience it. He spoke Latin and Rome sometimes paid his wages. But other than that, the centurion and the rest of the garrison were as British as the surviving native inhabitants. Mentally, Versillius had long decided to retire and prepare for the time when the western empire abandoned *Britannia* completely. This was something that he had seen about to happen for a while. In recent times, detachments of troops could be moved from Britannia , almost overnight, to the continent. There they might be sent to fight in *Dacia* or G*ermania* and meet their Romania end in a truly foreign field or forest. That prospect did not appeal to him in the slightest way.

    His own retirement villa was quite spacious, befitting his current rank. But it was not of such high status as the home of the prefect. For a start his villa was smaller and located at the rear of the eastern vicus. This was considered to be in a much less favoured position, than similar residences sited in the western vicus. Not the least because it did not have its own water supply, being too far from the natural spring. But it was closer to the public lavatories, baths and the eastern forum. Which meant that each day, he would have a shorter journey, to reach the essential communal facilities. Although the building was also closer to the thatched, plastered houses on the edge of the settlement, where the Britons and minor traders lived. They had the reputation of being less than pleasant and well-behaved neighbours. Much more to his liking, than his location and neighbours, was the fact that his villa was close to the tavern and house of pleasure. At the end of each night, he would have a much shorter walk, or stagger, home than somebody like the prefect.

    As they walked through the western vicus, with the fort behind them, Marcus finally broke his silence and said, awkwardly, "Gaius Flavius will not be most pleased if we rouse him at this time of the night. The prefect is well known for his bad temper and strong words."

Versillius knew that the young man was being diplomatic. but at the same time, he was obviously worried about jeopardising his own advancement in the legion. Gaius Flavius wielded great power, because of the importance of his office. Originally, a prefect had been a high-ranking military officer, with field responsibilities. In recent times, the role had changed, to become more about controlling the civic administration of Roman rule. Although he was still responsible for the *century* stationed in Virulanium. no young soldier would want to incur his easily and often demonstrated displeasure. The centurion was also aware that tongues were already wagging in the fort about his own impending retirement. Men were saying that the prospect of leaving the army had turned him soft - and he now spent too much time in the tavern or house of pleasure. As far as Versillius was concerned, they could gossip about him as much as they wanted, provided it was out of his earshot. He had, after all, almost served his full term and talk behind his back no longer worried him.

Marcus was seen by many as a potential candidate to succeed him as centurion, because of his acknowledged abilities and potential. This was despite his relative youth and lack of seniority. To a certain extent, it reflected quite badly on the standard of other men in the ranks. Because of this, Versillius wondered if the legionnaire might now be considering whether their association was potentially damaging to his career. Turning to the younger soldier, he answered, "I would have thought by now, that you must have realised that our profession is not always pleasurable. If we do not inform the prefect tonight, then we would only feel the even greater wrath of his tongue in the daylight. In my experience, it is usually better to get his admonishments out of the way sooner, rather than later. Besides he's not as much of a tyrant as he likes to pretend to be."

Marcus managed a half hearted smile, but made no other reply. By the time that Versillius had finished speaking, they had already reached the grounds of the prefect's villa. The two men made their way along the paved path, to the building's main entrance. The centurion banged heavily, several times, on the heavy wooden door. Eventually it was opened by the prefect's elderly slave, who was half asleep and carrying a small, oil lamp. The old man recognised Versillius in the glow of the flame, and asked tentatively, "Does this mean that I have to wake up the master and mistress?"

"Yes, I'm afraid so. We have grave news to tell him, which will not wait until the morning light," Versillius replied.

The flame from the lamp flickered, as the slave's shaking hand trembled at the prospect of disturbing his master. After breathing deeply, he half closed the door and walked slowly away from the entrance. He shook his head several times, as his feet carried him into the deep interior of the villa, towards the prefect's bedroom. The two soldiers watched his hesitant progress before following him. They then waited in a spacious antechamber, where Gaius Flavius normally received visitors. After a brief time, they heard a loud explosion of curses, which was then swiftly followed by the appearance of the prefect in his nightclothes. He was a short and portly man, in his mid fifties, who had long white hair and intense features. His legendary temper did not disappoint either legionnaire, as he rubbed his eyes and yelled, "Why in the name of Jupiter are you two fools here, at this time of night? You have disturbed my wife's sleep, for which no doubt, I will suffer greatly when you have gone. And as for my early meeting with the chief scribe tomorrow, that will be painful enough, without a decent night's sleep to fortify me!"

The days of polite greetings and respectful salutations had long since passed in Virulanium. After the onslaught had subsided, Versillius informed him about the discovery of Antonius' body, on his way back from the tavern. Marcus confirmed the details, from the time of his own involvement, before explaining that the watch had detected no sign of any intruders. The official looked shocked at their news and thought for a moment before saying, "Well, at least I can have a lie in tomorrow, as my meeting has obviously been cancelled. Not that even I would wish death on Antonius, merely to avoid spending a whole morning in his company. Now, tell me Versillius, who do you think is responsible for this crime?"

"It's too early to say, prefect. I've not really had a chance to get my thoughts into order..."

"Nonsense, man! It can only be the barbarians. A swift and silent incursion, resulting in the killing one of our people. No doubt they made a quick escape, when they saw you staggering back to the barracks, Versillius. Honestly, centurion, if you spent less time drinking and whoring, I'm sure that incidents of this nature would not occur!"

The centurion calmly let Gaius Flavius finish and responded, "Sir, drunk or not, I was wearing the very clothes that you see me in now. I doubt my toga and trousers would scare even the most timid of our northern neighbours into running away. If they were still on the scene at that time, then it is more than likely that you would have had two deaths in the settlement to contend with - rather than just the one. Besides, we have Marcus Pontius' statement that there were no incursions from the north."

"You may have a point there. So what, precisely, do you propose to do about this?" the prefect snapped back at him. But the tone in his voice was noticeably less belligerent, as he considered the implications of the centurion's words.

"Bear in mind that I discovered Antonius' body just inside the eastern forum, close to the fort's walls. So I suggest that we must mount an internal investigation into the incident. If this murder was committed by a member of the settlement, then it is as much your responsibility, as it is mine."

Again Gaius Flavius paused, as Marcus stood behind the centurion in respectful silence. Eventually, the official said, "Very well, officer, given the circumstances, I suppose that you must go ahead with such an enquiry. But please, try to keep it brief and unobtrusive. I have much important civic business to transact in the next few days. Besides, we wouldn't want anything to interfere with your impending retirement, would we?"

"Well, I certainly do not," Versillius responded, "But there is one more thing which I must request. I require the services of Marcus Pontius to assist me in this investigation. At my age, a man needs a younger pair of legs to do his running around."

The prefect smiled, an unusual event in itself, and said, "You are welcome to take him away from his normal duties. But just make sure that you spend more time on the enquiry than you normally pass in the tavern or the house of pleasure..." his voice suddenly tailed off. Then he approached the centurion, grasped his elbow and took him to one side. Finally, Gaius Flavius whispered confidentially, in a voice that was so low that not even Marcus could make out his words, "Tell me, Versillius, have they changed the girls in the brothel recently? It has been quite a while since I've been able to slip away..."

The centurion assured him that the turnover, in the house of pleasure, was as high as ever. A rueful expression creased the prefect's face and Versillius stifled a smile. Under civil Roman law a married man could commit adultery with impunity, if his mistress was unmarried or a prostitute. But in the prefect's household, domestic law held sway and took precedence. It boiled down to one very important point whether or not his wife, Juliana, might find out about his infidelities. And from his own experiences, Versillius knew that like her husband, Juliana was not a woman to be trifled with.

Having digested Versillius' news about the house of pleasure, Gaius Flavius ushered the centurion away and said, "You two can go now. But be sure to keep me informed. If we do have a murderer in Virulanium, then I want him caught and caught quickly!"

The centurion and Marcus then made their farewells and left the senior official to return to and placate his formidable spouse.

Chapter Three

The two men were both relieved to have got away so lightly at the prefect's villa. From his own perspective, Marcus could see that he had done his career prospects no harm. Versillius was also pleased because the younger man had been seconded to his investigation. The centurion had asked for Marcus' assistance because this was by no means the first murder enquiry that he had conducted. He always found that in such cases it was useful to have a junior colleague to bounce ideas off, as well as having somebody to do the legwork. Although, the Picts apart, Virulanium was usually a peaceful place. But on average there were two murders a year for the administration to deal with. The town had close to four hundred civilian inhabitants in the two *vicii*. There were also eighty legionnaires, a century or a sixth of a *cohort*, stationed in the fort. Because the surrounding settlement was so large, it acted as a magnet. Off duty, men from the surrounding towers and fortlets that spanned the Wall, joined with civilians from other vicii and descended upon Virulanium.

Every mile along the Wall's length there was a fortlet and every third of a mile a tower. Forts, like his own, were spaced every seven miles. But for some reason their vicus, on both the east and west of the forum, was larger than any other on the northern border. Perhaps, this popularity was due to the presence of the tavern and the house of pleasure, the centurion often told himself. Or maybe it was down to the number of coins that such a large number of people, many involved in trade, had circulating amongst them. And in Roman Britain good currency was everything. Without it no goods or produce could be obtained from the busy market place. "We'd better wake Artemis, the physician, from his slumbers," Versillius said, as they left the grounds surrounding the prefect's villa, "He may not be able to raise the dead scribe, but he can surely give us an expert opinion, as to the time and manner of the man's death."

Artemis lived in a small villa, on the western side of the vicus, not far away from the prefect. Unusually, for a community that was located on the northern border of the empire, he was of Greek origins. Versillius could only imagine that he liked the cold, damp weather in this part of the world. Alternatively, he thought that as a young man, the physician must have enjoyed travelling. But the doctor had now lived in the settlement for almost ten years and showed no sign of wanting to move on. Perhaps it was the cooler climate that he preferred to the heat of his native land. Unlike the prefect, Artemis owned no slaves, so the two men had to wait for the doctor himself to answer the door. Versillius apologised for rousing him at such a late hour and explained the reason for their visit. They then had to wait further, while he dressed, before he could accompany them back to the barracks. In contrast to the prefect, his temper was normally quite placid, but on this occasion he was quite short with them. As they left his villa, he said to Versillius, "Surely, this could have all waited until the morning? I mean the fellow is deceased isn't he? So I doubt there's much that I can do for him."

The centurion answered, "I need your opinion as to how long he has been dead and the manner of his death. After all, Artemis, this is a murder investigation when all is said and done. The sooner that the evidence is examined after death, the more chance that I have of catching the criminal."

"I'm sorry, for snapping at you, Versillius" the physician replied, as they walked together in the darkness, towards the fort's western gate, "But you must know that I couldn't stand the man. He was over officious and pompous to the highest degree, in my humble opinion as a citizen and a physician. Why, he even had the effrontery to criticise my methods of treatment on numerous occasions. What exactly does a scribe know about the practice of medicine, something that I have devoted my whole life to?"

The older soldier had to smile, because the slightly built, bald doctor was correct in his assessment of Antonius. The dead scribe had been a self appointed expert on every subject known to man. In the public amenities, where the citizens gathered, whatever issue was being discussed, he claimed to have just read this or that text relating to the very subject. Then he would go onto insist that his newly gained knowledge gave him the sole authority to speak on the topic. This was then done at great length and Antonius would haughtily dismiss any dissenting opinions. Most people in the settlement shared the physician's view of his arrogance and pomposity. Versillius also found it slightly amusing that the prefect's initial reaction to the murder had been one of relief that his meeting, with Antonius, was now unable to take place. By way of reply, he said to Artemis, "I'm not going to disagree with you. But we both have to put our personal feelings to one side. Antonius' murder has to be treated identically to that of any other member of our settlement."

This time it was the physician's turn to smile, as he said, "Put our feelings to one side, eh? Like the time when you threatened to pull his ginger beard out, clump by clump, after he told you about the 'correct' ways to construct a *ballista* and train your legionnaires?"

Fortunately, they reached the Western gate before Versillius could reply or Artemis could have another little outburst. The soldiers of the watch opened the gate, after recognising Marcus and the centurion. They had earlier deposited the body of the scribe in the main barracks building. It was laid out on a table, in a small side room, which was just inside the entrance to the barracks. The three men entered the torch lit room and after a brief examination, Artemis looked up and said, "A single stab wound to the stomach. He has probably been dead for almost four hours by now. Of course, were he still alive, then I dare say that he would give a much better diagnosis than I could. Now, can I go back to my bed, please?"

"What sort of an implement inflicted the wound?" Versillius asked, having already examined the incision for himself, while standing alongside the physician.

"A sword, in my opinion. It's far too large an entry wound for a dagger to have made. Yes, most definitely a sword. but I dare say, Versillius, that you had already deduced that..."

"I needed a second and professional opinion, Artemis. Unlike the deceased scribe, I do not flatter myself that I am qualified to speak on any matter with authority. And I thank you for your trouble and inconvenience." The centurion then indicated to the doctor that he could leave. As the physician departed, Versillius turned to Marcus and asked him, "What do you make of all this?"

"I cannot disagree with the physician. It does look like a sword did the job."

"But what sort of sword?" he countered, "Listen, I have had almost twenty five years experience of fighting and killing Picts. Give me your sword, please."

Puzzled at his request, the younger man handed over his *gladius,* the legionnaire's traditional, two foot long, stabbing weapon. Although this had largely fallen out of favour with most legionnaires, Versillius insisted that his century still carried it. Being a traditionalist, he had forbidden the use of the longer bladed *spatha*, by his men. Taking the sword from Marcus, he held it up in the torch light and said, "I know that the spatha is more than popular with most cohorts of the legion although it is not worn in Virulanium. But remember that the spatha is also a long, slashing sword, as favoured by the barbarians in these parts. The blow that killed the chief scribe was not inflicted by that type of weapon. A longer blade would have been aimed at and cut deeply into his neck or shoulder. Not his stomach."

He paused briefly and gently placed the tip of the gladius on the dead man's stomach. Marcus was surprised to see that width of the wound almost corresponded exactly with the breadth of his sword. Versillius then raised the weapon and pushed it forwards, towards Marcus in mock combat, saying, "And isn't this how we were taught to fight on the training grounds? Short, stabbing blows from behind the safety of our shields, straight into our opponents' stomachs or chests?"

The younger soldier digested his words, before replying, "You think that one of our own killed him, don't you, sir?"

"No, Marcus," he replied, "I don't think that. I know it. Look at the man's belt, have you noticed anything there?"

"No... should I have seen something?"

The centurion shook his head and grinned, thinking that maybe the younger man was not as clever as he had assumed him to be. Putting that thought to one side, he went onto say, "Exactly nothing is there and that is what you should have seen. Where is the man's purse and his civic keys? Why aren't they dangling from his belt? That alone proves that the Picts did not kill him. They have no use for our keys, coins and money. Only a Roman or Briton would want his money, as well as his life!"

"Unless one of the watch stole it, when they retrieved his body from the forum..."

"I doubt it, because although it was dark when I found the body, I rolled the scribe over to see who he was. While I was feeling for his wound, I cannot remember touching anything, beneath his toga. Mind you, it will do no harm for you to question your men in the morning. It will show them that you are on your toes. But there is at least one other thing that I do not understand..."

"What is that, sir?" the junior man replied.

"Why was Antonius out and about, from the warmth and comfort of his home, at that time of the night? It just seems to be so out of character. The man was better known for studying his ancient texts or modern papyrus writings from the continent, rather than visiting the forum that late at night. Unless, of course, he had arranged to meet his murderer."

"I can't disagree with you," Marcus said, as the centurion continued, "He must have been murdered just before I left the tavern to return to the barracks. If he had been killed any earlier, then my detachment of wall maintainers would have found his body, as they left some time before me. So why Antonius was in the forum so late and what he was doing there? It just makes no sense to me at the moment."

Marcus was again unable to suggest an answer. At this stage, Versillius decided that as the hour was late and they could accomplish nothing further that night. So it was time for him to sleep. Calling for the daytime watch commander, he made arrangements for the maintenance party to be sent out on their own, in the morning. He also told Marcus to meet him in the public baths, shortly after dawn broke. This would give the younger legionnaire a chance to question his men, before they could jointly decide how to take the murder case forwards. But as the young soldier showed no sign of wanting to leave, the centurion took one last glance at the dead man. It struck him that there was something else about the body that was not quite right. It took Versillius more than a few seconds to work out just what it was. Turning to Marcus, he said, "You were not the only person to miss something important tonight. I'm also being very slow as well. Look, the scribe's *intaglio* ring is no longer on his right hand..."

He was referring to a silver ring, which was inset with an oval of carved glass. Officials and citizens of note would impress the embossed glass into hot wax, to make a personal seal on the outside of their communications. It was actually regarded as a badge of office, for a senior servant of the civic administration.

"That's not exactly something that you would expect our illiterate, barbarian neighbours to have a great deal of use for!" he concluded, before heading for his bed and expecting Marcus to return to his duties.

Chapter Four

However, Marcus followed him through the barracks, all the way back towards his private quarters. Versillius was slightly confused by his behaviour and put it down to the lateness of the hour. As he reached the entrance to his rooms, Marcus placed his hand on the centurion's shoulder and whispered to him, "Sir, I'm sorry to intrude in such a manner. But I couldn't talk to you in the main part of the barracks. I realise that you want to talk in privacy, in the morning, but I have something to tell you now. Can we go inside your rooms, where we will be out of earshot from the rest of the garrison?"

Still puzzled, Versillius opened the door and led the junior man into his private rooms. After closing the door, he removed his *paenula*, the military cloak, and threw it on the floor. Then he collapsed on his bed and indicated a chair for Marcus to sit on. As the younger man sat down, the centurion asked, "What exactly do you have to tell me?"

The soldier swallowed and replied, "It's very difficult for me to put into words, sir. But now that I am seconded to your investigation..."

"No, Marcus, it is our investigation," the centurion interjected, "Our success, or failure, depends as much upon your involvement, as much as mine."

"Sorry sir, I put that incorrectly. I have some information that could assist us, although I am not entirely sure of its relevance."

"I'll decide that, if you can stop beating around the bush and spit it out!" Versillius answered, in a measured but firm manner. Unlike the prefect he knew that shouting loudly at subordinates was not very productive.

"It's about the cult of Mithras, centurion," Marcus replied, after a moment's hesitation, "Surely, you must have heard about the recent attempts to revive the religion, amongst the soldiers of our fort?"

"Of course I have. Now, please don't take this the wrong way, as I know that your father was an adherent of that religion. But I cannot see how the religious involvement of a few idiots and their silly rituals could be behind the murder of Antonius."

Marcus shook his head and said, "With respect, I think that you are wrong, sir. Two days ago, when I was walking through the Western forum, I overheard a conversation between Antonius and Trajanius. The chief scribe was threatening to take steps to initiate the proscription of Mithraism in Virulanium."

"Let me get this clear, Marcus. You are talking about our Trajanius, the legionnaire who was part of your watch tonight? The garrison's barrack room magistrate..."

"I'm afraid so centurion. He has been attempting to recruit members to the sect for several months. And I'm sorry to report that he has had some success with the men, but not with myself. Trajanius approached me because of my father's involvement with the sect, some twenty years ago. But I told him to go to Hades. I have no wish to stand in a dark pit, being paddled remorselessly, by my comrades."

Versillius rose to his feet and paced the room, before saying, "I can see that the proscription of the sect might give Trajanius a grudge against the scribe. But surely there must be more, if you suspect him of being involved in the murder?"

Again the younger man hesitated before replying, "There is nothing concrete. But remember where you found the chief scribe's body. It was between the western vicus and the southern wall. Trajanius was patrolling the southern side of the fort, on his own, until we heard your voice summoning our assistance."

"And I imagine that you are unable to say if he was present on the fort's wall, during the whole course of the evening," Versillius stated. As his subordinate shook his head, the centurion resumed, "Well, whether this is something or nothing, we had better speak with Trajanius about your suspicions. Let us do it now. Go and find him for me. Bring him to the ante room where Antonius' body is stored."

The centurion followed the young man out of his quarters and made his way to the antechamber. As he waited for the two soldiers to arrive, he refreshed his memory with his knowledge of Mithraism. Most of it had been gleaned some years ago, from Marcus' late father. He had been a very keen follower of the mystic cult. Mithras was originally an Indian god, whose worship had spread to Persia and from there, into the Roman Empire. The Persian manifestation of Mithras had portrayed him as the god of the sun. He had killed the primeval white bull to release its life force, for the benefit of humanity. The religion's emphasis on duty, courage and loyalty had appealed to many legionnaires. They had embraced the faith as a demonstration of their loyalty to the emperor. Despite its strange rituals and ordeals, the authorities had tolerated the army's obsession. This had lasted until Constantine I had taken to Christianity, almost forty years ago. From that point the cult had gone into decline, although every so often some dissatisfied soldier would attempt to foster its revival. And Trajanius was a man for whom the word "dissatisfied" might have been minted to describe. The legionnaire's disgruntled attitude was something that Versillius had experienced, at great cost to his well being, over his years in charge. But the centurion's thoughts were interrupted by the arrival of Marcus and Trajanius in the antechamber. Versillius acknowledged their presence and pointed to the body of Antonius, before stating, "Trajanius, I gather that our late scribe was not on the best of terms with you. Perhaps, this explains your earlier comments?"

The skinny soldier paused for a few moments, as the centurion awaited his reply. Trajanius was almost ten years younger than Versillius, but looked some years older than the centurion. His career in the army had been much less than spectacular. He had had never advanced above the lowest ranks of the legion and had a reputation for moaning and complaining second to none in Virulanium. Staring at his feet, rather than his commanding officer, he eventually answered saying, "He was a silly, old fool. That's what I said when he was alive and I'm not going to change my views, now that he's dead!"

The centurion grimaced at the man's disrespectful tone, but realising that Trajanius had long since been a lost cause said, "That's as maybe. But it just might be that you have some information about his murder. Anything that you can tell me would help the investigation. After all, you were patrolling the southern wall of the fort when he was killed, weren't you?"

"Not all night, I wasn't," the legionnaire retorted, "My stomach is upset and I had to obey several calls of nature. If you lot served us decent food, then I wouldn't have to visit the fort's *lavatorium* so often..."

Marcus finally lost his temper with the man's flippant replies, shouting at him, "How dare you desert your post without informing me! You are going to be put on a charge, legionnaire."

Trajanius was not prepared to be intimidated by Marcus. His attitude implied that he had seen keen, young watch commanders come and go. He shrugged his shoulders and answered, "I'd rather be put on a charge than parade around that southern wall with my trousers full of shit!"

Versillius stifled a smile and raised his arm to prevent Marcus from responding. As the younger man calmed down, the centurion approached Trajanius. He stopped when his face was less than a foot away from the soldier's face and said calmly, "You may soon have the opportunity to enjoy both experiences, if you continue to obstruct my enquiries. Now, tell me about your disagreement with Antonius and your involvement in the cult of Mithras. And that is a direct order from your commanding officer!"

"It is not a cult," Trajanius answered, as he fidgeted awkwardly with his hands, still avoiding direct eye contact, "It is the only true religion for a loyal soldier to follow. That dead idiot wanted to close us down, if we didn't pay him some taxes. I'd have killed him myself, if he had gone that far."

"Maybe you did," Versillius countered, "He was killed with a Roman sword. Just look at the wound. But I dare say that your gladius is nice and clean, isn't it, soldier? Just like it always is, no doubt..."

Trajanius nodded in reply, but still refused to make eye contact with the centurion or look at the dead man, as Versillius continued, "Now, get out of my sight and go back to your patrol on the wall. You will remain on duty for the rest of the night without leaving your post. And tomorrow, when your watch is done, you will take your trousers to Marcus. If the insides are not stained with your shit, then I will know that you have been lying to me about your stomach complaint. Then we will take this matter further. Understood?"

"Yes, sir!" was his barely audible reply, and it was uttered through tightly pursed lips. Trajanius knew that unlike Marcus, his centurion was not a man to be taken lightly.

"Well, get back to your duty then! The imperial army is not paying you to stand around idly!"

After the legionnaire had hurriedly departed, Versillius said to Marcus, "He's lying through his teeth, you know. Our current diet presents us with the opposite problem, rather than the one that he claimed to be suffering from. Make sure that he does bring you his breeches in the morning. I have a feeling that our most awkward and recalcitrant soldier is not telling us the entire truth."

Marcus grinned in acknowledgement of his comments and bade his superior officer a good night.

Chapter Five

The centurion only managed to snatch a few hours sleep before the sun rose and hid itself behind the high, dark clouds. Thoughts about the reasons behind the killing had swirled through his mind, preventing him from dozing off straight away. Still feeling tired, he put on his clothes and set off swiftly, towards the public amenities. But before he could resume the investigation, or meet Marcus by the pool, he had to perform his morning ablutions. On the way there, the rain that he had anticipated finally arrived, a thick and heavy drizzle. His first port of call was the communal lavatories, which were situated on the south eastern side of the forum. Although the barracks had both lavatories and a bathing area, he had specifically wanted to be outside of the military complex for his meeting with Marcus. Especially after his conversation with Trajanius.

The public latrines were arranged in four chambers of twelve seats. Each room had two parallel, stone benches, of six positions. The six positions were holes that had been cut into the stone. Luckily for Versillius, one of the twelve seats in his normal chamber was vacant. The centurion was starting to get quite desperate, by the time that he had crossed the eastern forum. Assuming the vacant seat, he swiftly lowered his trousers, hitched up his tunica and sat down. On his right hand side was Vespasianus the merchant, and on his left Paribius the money lender. They greeted him in the customary, jovial fashion, which was always prevalent amongst the men, in the settlement's shared toilet facilities. With the greetings over they then resumed the interrupted conversations with their neighbours.

Versillius made himself comfortable and remained silent, preferring to listen to their chatter and concentrate on the job in hand. But just at the moment when the centurion was half way through squeezing out a particularly hard turd, Vespasianus looked around and said to him, "The whole town is taking about the murder of this scribe fellow. Is it true that you're the man in charge of the investigation?"

The merchant was a thin, olive skinned man known for his business acumen. "Just give me one second," Versillius replied, his mind elsewhere, as he unclenched his buttock cheeks, and pushed firmly. The stool plopped out and the feeling of relief was instantaneous. Reaching behind him, he sighed and took up a handful of moist leaves. This was what they were reduced to using now that the supply of sponges from the Mediterranean had ceased. While he was wiping his bottom, the centurion said, "That's much better. Now, Vespasianus, what was it that you asked me?"

The merchant repeated his question. Other than the odd burst of flatulence, the lavatory was now quiet, as the men awaited his reply. Versillius noticed the sudden silence and replied, "As our settlement's centurion it is my job to locate his murderer. Surely, you must all know that?"

"Well, you'll certainly have enough suspects," Paribius cut in, as he himself released a huge log, the size of which brought tears to his eyes. The tall dark, haired money lender caught his breath for a few seconds, before continuing, "Oh, goodness me, that hurt somewhat! Now, where was I? Ah, yes, the scribe. Let me tell you, Versillius, that nobody in the town had any time for him. He was just a jumped up, petty, little official, living in a nice villa that was paid for by our taxes! "

Falling silent, Paribius reached behind for himself some leaves, but then suddenly appeared to think better of it, saying, "Hang on boys, there's another one on the way. I think this could break the turd pit into two pieces. Hold your noses chaps, here it comes!"

His words were followed by a loud groan and the men all laughed, apart from Versillius. It was not that he found lavatorial humour unfunny. Under normal circumstances he could sit and pass wind alongside the best of them, particularly given the amount of beer that he drank. But the centurion had just realised that he was emptying his bowels next to two people who might have a motive for killing Antonius. Both Paribius and Vespasianus had recently disagreed acrimoniously with the scribe, after he had publicly threatened to revoke their licences for trading. The argument had centred around the proposed increased licence fees and rents for their premises. But before he could consider the matter any further, the money lender took centre stage again. This time he half rose and shouted, in the act of vigorously forcing another stool out, "By Jupiter, you could load this one into a siege machine and breach a fortification stronger than anything even the emperor Hadrian ever built. I'm going to have to speak to my wife and mistress, about what they are feeding me with. My poor arse can't take this sort of punishment for much longer."

"Tell that to your boyfriend," a voice cried out, from the rear of the lavatory.

Ignoring the heckler, Paribius finished squeezing the massive turd out, while at the same time, he pointed his wrinkled cock into the pit, and started to urinate saying, "Who says that you can't piss and shit at the same time? I think that I've just proved them wrong, whoever they were!"

Amidst much ribald laughter, followed by further comments about his sexual orientation and liaisons with young men, he then sat down. With his motions now finished, the money lender was finally able to reach for the soothing leaves. Personally, Versillius ascribed the firmness of their turds to the lack of olive oil and good red wine. Constipation seemed to have become a common complaint in recent times, shared by both the soldiers and citizens of the settlement. All of his life, the centurion had been used to plentiful imports of well filled *amphorae* from the continent. But since the turn of the year, such shipments, like the men's turds, had either dried up or had not been reaching the far north. He saw the lack of such luxury goods from the empire as yet another sign of Rome's ties to the provinces beginning to loosen. It was for this very reason that he had refused to accept Trajanius' story about suffering from loose bowels, while on duty. Thinking about the recalcitrant soldier triggered another thought in his mind. He remembered a fact that he had been trying to recall about Mithraism, from the previous night. In its original manifestation the cult had not only appealed to legionnaires, but also to merchants and market traders.

As the centurion had completed his own ablutions, he rose and pulled up his trousers. Domitius, who owned a shop in the forum and was sat on the bench directly opposite him said, "So you're not staying long today, centurion. This murder business must be playing on your mind. I do not envy your problem, Paribius was quite right. You will find very few people in Virulanium who held a high opinion of Antonius the scribe."

Most Roman men were quite happy to spend up to an hour in the communal toilets, talking with their friends, before going into the bathhouses. Apart from the smell, Versillius had no problems with that under normal circumstances. Even in the fort's latrines, such behaviour and companionship was not unknown. But as he had arranged to meet Marcus in the baths, he made his farewells and left them to chat the morning away. Although he did recall that even Domitius had also recently fallen out with Antonius. This was over civic demands for an increased rent, on his trader's shop in the forum and licence to conduct business. At this rate, it was going to be easier to find a virgin working in the house of pleasure, than somebody in Virulanium who held no grudge against the dead man.

"Our friend, Domitius speaks nothing less than the truth," Vespasianus stated, as the centurion walked towards the exit, which led to the bathhouses. When Versillius turned, to catch his words, the merchant resumed, saying, "But some people might even consider you, or one of your men, to be a suspect. How much money has the scribe withheld from your pay in recent months?"

Chapter Six

After ignoring Vespasianus' comments and leaving the communal lavatories, the centurion walked through the short corridor to the public baths. He entered through the vestibule, where the tessellated floor bore the inscription, "Enter, Friend and be cleansed. Remember Octavian Petronius as you bathe." The reference was a tribute from a rich patron, who two generations ago, had funded the building of this much needed public facility. It was a well-appointed *basilica,* which had an excellent *calderium* and *frigidaria*. Despite the constant rainfall in the northern outpost, only the fort and western villas had water supplied to them. This came from a spring, which rose at the top of the western vicus. The source had a limited capability, so all the other residences in Virulanium did not have their own water or sewerage supply. Hence the settlement's need for shared latrines, baths and the public fountains. Virulanium's nearest river was located to the south of the settlement, on lower ground. It had been a tremendous feat of engineering, by the old legions, to bring water to the public amenities. Fresh water was channelled by underground piping, to specially constructed aquifers. Then pressure caused by the constant flow of water from the river, forced the supply in the aquifers above ground.

Leaving the greeting from Petronius behind, Versillius crossed the ornate mosaics. As always, he glanced at the images of the gods and imaginary beasts in their bright colours, before entering a small side room. There he undressed and wrapped a woven, linen towel around his waist. The centurion then left the vestibule and walked through the shallow foot pool, where he bathed his feet. Although the water was cold, the room, one of two on either side of the approach to the pool, was warm. This was because the foot baths were located next to the *hypocaust*, which supplied both the under floor and internal wall heating to the hot or warm rooms. Due to the constant supply of hot steam, from the hypocaust, the bathhouse had been built with a solid tiled roof. A wooden roof would have rotted away many years ago. This was unlike the public lavatory next door, which had a thatched roof, to supply the citizens with much needed ventilation. With his feet now cleansed, Versillius approached a basin and washed his hands and face. It was accepted form that users of the facilities did not enter the main part of the baths with excessive dirt on their person.

Of course such high status civic amenities were only available to middle or top ranking members of the local community. Anybody who lived in a low status round house, or was enslaved, did not have access to these facilities. They had to make do with the nearest river for bathing or for disposing of their solid toilet. But even the waste from the shared public latrines ended up in the river. This was some thing that the centurion had always found confusing; if the drinking water came from the same water supply, just how clean could it be? Perhaps, he thought to himself, this was the real reason why he drank so much beer. Or even red wine, when it was available in Virulanium. It was his considered view that the purity of both fermented liquids was guaranteed, unlike that of their drinking water.

In the central room of the bathhouse, which housed the swimming pool, Marcus was already present. This was a warm, as opposed to a hot or medium chamber. The younger soldier had recently been in the water and was now having aromatic oils rubbed into his skin, by attendants. Versillius greeted him and then moved into the calderium, or hot room saying, "Sorry, for being a little bit on the late side. I'll be back with you in a moment. But I just need to steam the stench of the communal lavatories from my body first."

Marcus acknowledged his comments, with a wave of his hand, as he was no doubt enjoying the pleasant sensation of having his body massaged. Versillius was true to his word and did not remain for long in the calderium, just a sufficient time to open his skin's pores. He returned to the warm room and after removing his towel, dived into the pool. The centurion found the cool water to his satisfaction, after the steam of the hot room and swam several lengths before returning to his subordinate. Feeling refreshed and now more than half awake, he stretched out his stocky frame on the covered couch and relaxed. As the second attendant rubbed the scented oils into his flesh, he said to Marcus, "We'd better talk now, as we are on our own. My group of acquaintances from the lavatory will be here soon. I've already identified three of their number, who have recently had financial disagreements with the scribe."

"Only that many?" Marcus replied, "Off the top of my head, I can't think of a man who was more unpopular in Virulanium."

The centurion sighed with pleasure, as he lay face down, enjoying the feel and smell of the herbal lotions being rubbed into his shoulders. He said, "We must also remember that as well as being our chief scribe, Antonius was the town's de facto tax collector. As the prefect's senior civic official, he charged the traders their licence fees and was responsible for levying taxes on them and the likes of you and me. In our case, he was also responsible for deciding how much of our pay should be withheld. And as a sideline, he was also a self appointed expert on every topic under the sun. Taking all of that into account, do you think he was likely to be popular?"

Marcus responded, "I know what you are saying, sir. But from my own dealings with Antonius, he seemed to positively relish his unpopularity."

"But that was the man, soldier, he was never prepared to be proved wrong or give ground on official or other matters. Now, leaving that to one side, where do you think we should start our investigation?"

"Well, not with your three friends from the lavatory, centurion. With respect, I'd prefer to start with the priestess, Drusilla. It is commonly known that the scribe had recently filed a writ for the seizure of the temple's assets, using Constantine the First's dictum of Milan, as his justification." Versillius was again impressed by the young man's knowledge and perception. He hadn't initially considered the potential involvement of the priestess, who had more than enough reason to dislike the scribe. Constantine I, the late emperor, had made Christianity the main religion of the empire, after his victory at Milvian Bridge. Pagan worship had then gone into decline. His successors, and unscrupulous local officials, had subsequently decreed that the wealth of pagan temples be seized by the state. But being so far from Rome, the old ways of worship were still practised with impunity in the north. Even the cult of Mithras had been tolerated, if not approved of. It was also common knowledge that Virulanium's temple was still very wealthy, having been established for over two hundred years. However, Antonius had recently applied to the governor for the religious dicta to be applied against the temple. This would mean that its assets could be confiscated and the building closed down. That struck the centurion as a sufficient reason to annoy the high priestess. She might soon find herself out of a job, and without a *denarius* to her name.

The other issue that it explained was Antonius' run in with Trajanius. The chief scribe might have been over officious, but he was usually even handed in his dealings with people. Like the centurion, he would have been aware of the attempted revival of Mithraism. But he would not have proceeded against the temple of Jupiter, without bringing similar strictures to bear against the cult. Having weighed these thoughts in his mind, Versillius said, "Of course, the priestess could not have wielded the sword. But you are right in your thinking. Drusilla had a good enough motive to get somebody else to deal the fatal blow to the scribe. But this line of enquiry does not help us to explain Trajanius' potential involvement. Setting himself up as a rival to the temple would not endear him to the priestess. I can hardly see those two acting in an unholy alliance."

"I agree, sir," Marcus replied, "But talking of Trajanius, before I left the fort he brought me his trousers. He seemed very pleased with the fact that they were soiled, after his night's duties."

"Whether his so called illness took its course, or he deliberately fouled himself is another question. Knowing the man as I do, my money is on the latter!" Then hearing some noise from the vestibule, the centurion went onto say, "We'd better get a move on, I think my so called friends are here. Do you fancy a quick dip in the frigidaria, before we put our clothes back...?"

Before he could finish, a loud voice interrupted him. As he had suspected, it was Paribius and the rest of the crowd from the communal lavatory. The money lender announced his arrival in the warm room, by saying loudly, "Bring me your finest oils, attendants! After this morning's gruesome toilet, my sore rectum is in great and dire need of their soothing qualities!"

The slave, who was massaging Versillius, closed his eyes, as an expression of extreme distaste registered on his face. Marcus's attendant swallowed heavily and squeezed the young soldier's shoulders, just a little bit more tightly than he should have done and then shuddered. Paribius, totally ignorant of the attendants looks of disgust, ripped off his towel and leapt into the pool shouting, "When it's cleaned and oiled, boys, you're all welcome to queue up and kiss it..."

Chapter Seven

The two soldiers had a quick dip in the cold pool, or frigidaria, before dressing and leaving the public baths. Their destination, the temple of Jupiter, was situated in the western forum, directly in front of the fountain. It took only a short walk across the southern road, until they reached the handsome portico, or the front of the building. But to Versillius' trained eye, honed by years of maintaining the Wall, it was obvious that the structure was now in need of some repair. The once bright paint that decorated the architrave and its supporting pillars had long faded, eroded by the harsh, northern weather. Similarly, the mortar between many of the stone blocks, on all sides of the building, was crumbling away. Since the Christians had been allowed to build their wooden church, on the western side of the settlement, attendance at the pagan temple had been in decline.

But despite the building's shabby appearance, Versillius like Antonius before him, was not fooled. The institution was undoubtedly still very wealthy, having been in receipt of votive offerings and donations for well over two centuries. Visible evidence of this decorated the building's external walls. Over the years, many legionnaires had paid good money to the temple, for the carving of dedications into its stone blocks. Most proclaimed their originators' devotion to Jupiter or loyalty to the ruling emperor. But occasionally, there was a sentiment that echoed across the years. One soldier, Varus Aquilius, gave thanks for his child's recovery from illness. Another, Gallus Marullinus, proclaimed his gratitude at being promoted to the rank of centurion. Versillius knew that both of these men had been dead for more than a hundred years, but their carvings still spoke poignantly on their behalf.

Leading the way, he entered the temple, for the first time in many years. Then the two soldiers walked into a plain entrance room and Versillius called for Drusilla, the high priestess. After a few moments, she appeared from inside the main chamber and said, "This is a surprise, centurion. I am unable to remember the last time that you worshipped here. Although, perhaps you and your young friend have lost your bearings, Versillius. Caracalla's tavern is a little further to the east, outside the city walls!" Drusilla was still a handsome woman, despite being in her early forties. Her high cheek bones and pert breasts had seduced many a young legionnaire, in his dreams. But the centurion thought that her most attractive feature was her beautiful long, dark hair. It was always tied up into a tight bun and decorated with several ornate, silver hairpins. Unfortunately, the priestess also possessed an extremely bitter tongue, which she was not afraid to use. The centurion had long considered that her vocation, which prevented her from taking a husband, must surely have saved some man from a life of absolute misery.

He replied, "We need to speak with you, Drusilla. I am here on official business."

"So am I," she answered nonchalantly, walking away from them, back towards the dark interior of the building, "But if you wish to come through to the main chamber, then you must cleanse yourselves first."

"We have only just come from the public bath houses," Marcus said.

Versillius knew that the priestess would not be persuaded by such an argument. He was not disappointed, because she turned around and answered, "There is water in the large bowl and as you have crossed the forum, I suggest that you use it. The gods do not want the dust on your hands and feet to soil this sacred place. When you are finished, I will expect you to make a small donation. The bowl does not refill itself with water." Drusilla then turned away and departed from the entrance room, back into the main part of the temple. Marcus and Versillius smiled at each other and realised that as they needed to question the priestess, approached the bowl. They washed their hands and brushed down their feet. After dropping two small coins onto the collection plate, the two men entered the inner sanctum. The main statue of Jupiter was positioned at the rear of the room. Along the approach, placed in recesses, were several smaller statues of the other deities. The centurion recognised the images of Mars, Venus and Minerva. He also noticed that the floor beneath his feet had been clumsily repaired. Where the mosaic had been worn away or cracked, the resulting gaps had been filled with plaster, rather than replaced with the small, delicately crafted *tesserae*.

Drusilla was stood behind a side altar, arranging five miniature statues of late emperors, on its surface. Until Constantine's edicts, living imperial rulers had always been universally regarded as deities throughout the empire. Even in death, more popular emperors were still worshipped. Where the old religion was followed this practice continued. But as the centurion told himself, it was hard to worship the current ruler Magnentius. Especially as not a single coin bearing his image had yet been seen in Virulanium. Walking towards the priestess, he said, "I'm sure that you know my subordinate, Marcus Pontius. I am also sure that you know exactly why we are here."

She shook her head and having finished placing the images on the altar, looked up and replied, "Could it possibly have something to do with the death of the much loathed scribe? Not that I would know anything about his timely demise. So you are wasting your time in here, centurion!"

Versillius let her finish and then tried to steer the conversation back to the reason for his visit saying, "I may be wasting my time. But I am here to ask you about the man who was trying to sequester your temple's assets and put you out of a job. I'd have thought that would be motive enough for anybody to want him dead."

Drusilla laughed and picked up a statue of Claudius from the altar. After examining it closely, she went onto reply, "I'll admit that I wanted him gone. But you need to speak to the deities rather than to myself. After all, it was they who answered my prayers. I can tell you no more, that is, unless you wish me to seek guidance from the true gods. Of course, I'm more that prepared to do that, provided you make an appropriate offering."

As she finished, Marcus moved forwards and asked her, "Do the gods wield a gladius, priestess, and kill mortal men? I thought thunderbolts from Mount Olympus were more their style."

Drusilla turned to face him and angrily stated, "Soldier, I strongly suggest that you do not joke about the power of the deities. They have already sent one man to the underworld. Take care that you do not follow him before your time, young man!"

"Neither myself or my colleague, have any intention of doing that," Versillius countered, "But we will find out who was responsible for the murder and ensure that he or she is brought to justice. Tell me, what do you know about the revival of the cult of Mithras in Virulanium?"

"Nothing but the fact that some of your silly soldiers are involved," she replied, "Can you imagine anything more ridiculous than grown men standing naked in a dark pit, while they are beaten senseless with wooden paddles or worse? Sometimes, I think that you legionnaires have no sense whatsoever!"

The centurion could see that this interview would yield no further results, so he said, "We will leave you to your ceremonial duties. But I will be pursuing this investigation to its conclusion. Rest assured Drusilla, that if I find that you are involved in any way, then neither Jupiter or your office of high priestess will offer you any protection whatsoever."

Drusilla was not pleased with his words. Even in the half light, Versillius caught the flash of anger in her dark, brown eyes, as she yelled back at him, "I do not need my position to protect me, centurion! There are more powerful forces than you can ever imagine looking after my interests and those of the temple."

The two men shrugged at her outburst and leaving the building, walked back into the forum.

Chapter Eight

The market was quite crowded and bustling with shoppers and traders, when the two men left the temple and walked across to the eastern forum. As this was the second day after the weekend, people from the outlying farms and settlements had gradually made their way to Virulanium. They had goods to sell to Vespasianus and produce to purchase from the traders. And there were only two trading days remaining before the fifth or rest day. This was when Virulanium came to a halt, as the market traders and merchants took a day of rest. After noting, with some relief, that the drizzle had stopped, Marcus said to his superior, "We didn't get very far with the high priestess, sir. I'm sorry if my words provoked her and made you terminate the interview early."

Versillius grinned back at him and said, "I was almost ready to leave before you spoke. Anyway, the chances of her breaking down and making a confession were remote. As you no doubt observed, she's a very difficult woman. The main reason for our visit was to let Drusilla know that she is on our list of suspects. I think that objective was achieved, for the small cost of incurring her displeasure."

The centurion then suggested that they took time to eat, from one of the food vendors in the market place. He had already decided that their next visit would be to question Paribius. Versillius knew that the money lender would not be finished at the bathhouses yet. Like his visits to the lavatory, Paribius enjoyed lingering at the poolside, before dressing and conducting his business after lunchtime. So the two legionnaires ate a late breakfast of thinly sliced bread, stuffed with a mixture of finely minced beef and onions. They sat eating and waiting, outside the office in the forum, where Paribius carried out his trade. Marcus, who was now feeling more relaxed in the company of his senior officer, said by way of making conversation, "Can I ask you about this immense wall, that we spend our life guarding and repairing? It strikes me that it is not very good at keeping the Picts out. I'm not saying that the barbarians killed Antonius. But they do seem to be able to cross the border, whenever it suits them. Whatever we do to try and stop them seems to have no effect."

"Who said that the Wall was constructed to keep the barbarians out?" Versillius replied, "It was built to keep us in. The emperor Hadrian set the ultimate boundaries of the empire well over three centuries ago. Since that time, there have been no further imperial conquests. Do you realise that when the wall was built we had three whole legions in Britain? Now we have barely one, our own, just what is left of the twentieth. And that is now much less than five thousand men."

During recent years there had been a large transfer of soldiers serving in the northern outpost, to the continent. These demands had intensified as the imperial boundaries came under increasing attack from the continental barbarians. In the centurion's view the troop withdrawals added to his feelings of foreboding. Britannia and the twentieth legion were being cut adrift from their supposed homeland. Marcus, who by now had finished his food, asked, "Three whole legions! Compared to our total complement that seems like a lot of men. What did they do?"

"They built a bloody great wall, from the east coast to the west. And when that was done our leaders made them build hundreds of miles of roads for good measure. It was an ideal way of keeping the army occupied and out of mischief," Versillius responded, with just a trace of cynicism in his voice. He swallowed the last mouthful of his bread and mince before continuing, "By the way, Marcus, please don't take this as a criticism, but your grasp of our history appears to be somewhat lacking!"

The younger man hesitated before saying, "I'm sorry, sir. But it's not entirely my fault. Perhaps, you can recall the name of the person who instructed me on these matters, when I joined the army?"

Versillius did not respond, knowing full well that he was the person that Marcus was referring to. But both the young soldier's history lesson and the centurion's embarrassment were interrupted by the arrival of Paribius. The money lender looked freshly cleansed and oiled, after his visit to the bathhouse. The two soldiers watched, as he strolled jauntily through the crowd, whistling to himself. His tall frame exuded confidence, which was reinforced by thick, dark hair and a closely cropped beard. Versillius believed him to be around thirty five years old. However, Paribius' normally ruddy complexion instantly turned pale, when he saw the two legionnaires sat outside his office. Focusing directly on the centurion, he said, "Unless you are both short of money, then I suppose that this is has to be an official visit. You're here about Antonius, aren't you?"

"You are not the only one that we have to question, Paribius. Perhaps it would be better if we went inside, where there is less chance of us being overheard?" Versillius replied, as he rose to his feet.

Looking rather glum and definitely less jaunty, Paribius unlocked his office door and ushered the two men in, saying to them, "Listen, Versillius, I may have been talking out of turn in the lavatories earlier. All I did was to report what the whole town is saying about

Antonius. And I'm sure that Vespasianus meant nothing when he spoke about your pay being docked..."

The centurion did not let him finish saying, "Let us forget what was said in the lavatorium, especially your overall contribution to the proceedings. But I know that the scribe had threatened to revoke your money lender's licence, if you refused to pay the increased taxes. And there was also the matter of the rent rise. Without your licence or office you would have no profession. Some might see that as a reason for murder."

Paribius blanched visibly and replied, "It was just a simple disagreement over the constant increases that he was demanding from me and the other traders. Come on, you know what it is like in Virulanium now! All of us, soldiers or civilians alike, are struggling to make a living. When was the last time that a shipment of freshly minted coins arrived from Rome?"

"Are you able to you vouch for your whereabouts, last night?" Marcus asked him, ignoring the money lender's pleas.

"Of course I can," was the reply, "I was with Vespasianus and Domitius, in the merchant's villa. Oh, dear me, we...we were discussing ways of resisting the licence and rent increases. I suppose that sounds rather bad, doesn't it?"

Versillius let the man's voice tail off and thought for a moment, before saying, "Where is your tally list of debtors, Paribius? I need to see it."

"I don't need to show it to you, centurion. Although, of course, you are more than welcome to see it. But I'll tell you now, that like a lot of people, Antonius owed me money. Where do you think he got the finance to purchase his villa? Not everybody in Virulanium can afford to pay cash, like you did!"

"And was he behind in his payments?" Marcus cut in.

"I suppose he was, by a month or so. But given the settlement's circumstances most of my clients are. Money lending is no longer such a profitable trade as it once was. To be honest, I don't even know why I do it any longer, as I barely cover my costs. Anyway, Versillius, have you ever known me harm one single member of this community over the late repayment of a debt? That is not the way that I do business!" the money lender replied, very emphatically.

"No, but there is always a first time for everything," the centurion responded, "Especially as Antonius was unmarried and without children. Because of his outstanding debt, the law will now give you full title to the property and land that the scribe purchased..."

"Look, I didn't have anything to do with his death. Please, ask Vespasianus and Domitius. They'll confirm my story and vouch for my whereabouts last night."

"We will be talking to them very shortly," Versillius assured him, before gesturing to Marcus that the interview with Paribius was now done. Leaving the money lender to lower himself gingerly into a chair, the two men left his office. Observing his disposition, the centurion thought to himself about the problems, which Paribius had earlier described at great length in the latrines. They could not been entirely resolved by the application of bathing oils. Unless it was their visit that had caused him such obvious and painful discomfort, as he sat himself down.

Chapter Nine

Outside in the forum it was raining again, something that seemed to happen several times a day in Virulanium, even in the summer months. Marcus could see that the centurion was thinking hard, but felt confident enough to ask, "Although he was better tempered than the priestess, we didn't learn a great deal in there, did we, sir?"

Versillius shook his head and replied, "Not much, apart from the fact that the scribe was an honest man. As the tax collector, he had access to the town's revenues. But he owed money to Paribius, for the purchase of his villa. So Antonius could not have been a corrupt official, especially as he was a month behind in his loan repayments. I also learnt that he was a stupid and scrupulous man. If you were in debt to Paribius and owed him a substantial sum of money, would you publicly threaten to revoke the money lender's licence?"

"Everybody says that the man was terribly officious. And you have already told me that it was his nature to apply the strict letter of the law. But I understand your point about his honesty."

Versillius did not answer him, because they had almost reached the shop where Domitius traded. He sold fresh produce from the fields; fruits, vegetables and roots. As they approached his premises, the centurion pulled Marcus to one side and said, "Listen, don't let this man fool you. He's a lot shrewder than Paribius who, as you may have gathered, is our resident clown. Domitius does not say a lot, but when he speaks, his words are usually worth listening to. Even if they are a little on the pointed side."

Like the money lender, the shopkeeper seemed less than pleased to see the two soldiers enter his premises. The trader was a thin, grey haired man in his early sixties. His sunken cheeks and pointed nose gave him an aquiline appearance. After leading Marcus and Versillius into the back of the shop, he said, "I know why you are here, but the pair of you have made a wasted journey. Haven't you got better things to do than disrupt my trade?"

"I'm sorry, Domitius, but we are investigating a murder. Perhaps, you would prefer to answer our questions in the barracks, rather than here?" the centurion replied, refusing to be intimidated.

"Ask me what ever you like, but be brief about it. I spent the whole of last night with Paribius and Vespasianus, they will vouch for me."

"We have already been told that the three of you were discussing ways of avoiding the increased taxes that Antonius was about to levy. Something that you all found to be a particularly sore subject?" Marcus asked.

"Yes, we spent the night together, planning our appeal to the governor. As far as I know, that is not yet an illegal activity," the shopkeeper retorted, somewhat angrily.

"But murder is," the centurion stated firmly, "And be certain that I will get to the bottom of this matter. Of course, if you are innocent of involvement in this crime, then you have nothing to fear. Neither from myself, or anybody else, who enforces the law. But maybe you have some information that could help me to solve this murder? That could help you, if you don't leave things for too long. For instance, I understand that a revival of the worship of Mithras is taking place in Virulanium. Would you know anything about that?"

"I can see what you are implying, centurion. But you are still wasting your time. We traders have long discarded that old cult. Round bits of precious metal, bearing the image of an emperor, are much more to my taste than religion."

"Even if more of them have to be handed over to Antonius?" Without waiting for a reply, Versillius turned to his subordinate and continued, "Come, Marcus, we must go and question the merchant, Vespasianus. Let us see if his story backs up that of his two colleagues." The centurion hated investigations of this nature. When they were concluded and the perpetrator was apprehended, all the other suspects in such a case bore a grudge against him. In this small, communal society, where even lavatories and baths were shared, it made his life very difficult. Roll on retirement, he thought to himself, as they left Domitius's shop to search out the merchant.

Outside in the market place, Marcus kept his silence. He had already realised that the centurion seemed to notice and perceive far more than he did from the suspects. This view had been especially reinforced after his analysis of their interview with Paribius. But remembering the older man's seniority and greater experience, the legionnaire knew that he could only learn from him. Besides, he was more than pleased that the officer had requested his secondment to the enquiry. Working alongside the centurion could do his promotion prospects no harm, when the older man retired. Once they were some distance from Domitius' shop Versillius said, "I've saved the best for last. Vespasianus is the brains behind this triumvirate. The other two rely on him for almost everything."

"So then it is highly unlikely that we'll get anything out of him, is it sir?" Marcus replied. They then walked through the forum, trying to find the wholesale merchant. Vespasianus controlled the supply of almost all the goods that were on sale. Although he held no official title, his role was effectively that of market superintendent. It did not take them long to trace him. The merchant was stood in the middle of the public piazza, berating a stall holder about the late payment of a bill, saying to him, "I'm not made of money, man. None of us are in these times! Now, you must pay up what you owe me, or you will get no more supplies from my warehouse. Do you understand?"

The market trader bowed his head awkwardly, and answered, "But I have offered you payment, excellency. Please, take this bag of coins. It's payment in full."

Vespasianus was a tall man, who towered over the stall holder. His olive complexion seemed incongruous on the Northern frontier. Using his height to intimidate the smaller man, he placed his hands on his hips and shouted,
"Bull's shit! You have offered me nothing more than a bag of bull's shit. Those coins are gold plated and bear the image of the emperor Constans. As he is dead, they are now totally worthless. Bring me coins of gold or silver *solidus* and then we can do business. Until then, forget it!"

But before the supplicant could reply, the merchant glanced up and saw the two soldiers approaching him. Turning to the trader, he said, "I'll finish this conversation with you later. It looks as if I have more pressing matters to deal with." The stall holder walked away, glad to be spared any further ear bashing for the moment.

"Shall we go to your office, Vespasianus?" the centurion asked.

"If we have to. But listen to me Versillius, doesn't your so called imperial army, have anything more useful to do than harass innocent traders and merchants? Remember that my taxes pay your wages," he replied, as he led them to his office, which was sited on the western side of the forum. The centurion chose not to answer his question directly. He waited until they were out of the open and sat in Vespasianus' rooms, before saying, "Vespasianus, you must realise that I am only doing my duty. When a man has been murdered then I must make enquiries, however unpleasant that may be for the two of us. I'm only here to find out about your whereabouts last night."

"As I am sure that you have previously spoken to Paribius and Domitius, then you will be aware of our movements already. We were in my villa, drafting our petition to the governor about the exorbitant licence and tax increases. Why, if you had been at your own home, you would have seen my lights burning late into the night."

This could have been true, because the merchant's property was sited just in front of the centurion's retirement home. But Versillius asked him, "Are you sure that your meeting was not of a religious nature? There appears to be something of a revival in the worship of Mithras taking place in the settlement."

Vespasianus barely hesitated before laughing and then replying, "That is more likely to be your problem than mine. Talk to your legionnaire Trajanius. The fool approached me some weeks ago. Apparently, I am a market trader and therefore owe allegiance to Mithras. He claimed to be at the sixth level of devotion and a *heliodromus* and could introduce me to the master at any time! As to what a heliodromus is, I certainly do not have a clue."

"Did he tell you the name of the master?" Marcus asked him, "And a heliodromus is a runner of the sun. It's the sixth level of the cult, one below the *pater* or master. My late father used to be a follower..."

"Well, now I know. But as for the pater, that was going to wait, until I had sworn eternal allegiance and undergone five levels of the most severe ordeals. I respectfully declined his kind offer and threatened to report him to the prefect. At that point he seemed to loose any interest in recruiting me. But I fail to see what this has to do with the death of Antonius."

Versillius answered, "The scribe was rather heavy handed in dealing with many groups in the community, not only traders and merchants. But getting back to last night, at what time did you stop working on the petition?"

"Around the time that I heard your voice bellowing for the watch. I was standing outside, saying good night to my guests. You must know that noise carries very easily at that time of the night. My wife can verify that neither I, or the other two, left the villa until after the scribe was killed."

The centurion looked up at him and said, "I'd like to believe you Vespasianus and your story certainly sounds convincing. But just remember, that I've broken alibis before. I hope that you are telling the truth. Perhaps you could show me this petition, which the three of you have put so much work into? It would tidy things up nicely."

"I don't have it here, it's in my villa. If you really need to see it, feel free to call round at any time. You can come round tonight, if you want to. We'll be there, working on the finishing touches to the document. There can be no doubt that when the governor receives it, he will have no alternative but to reverse the increases. Antonius himself could not have drafted a better set of arguments."

"I will probably take you up on that offer, merchant. But just one more question, did the scribe owe you any money for goods or services?" Versillius asked.

"No more than anybody else in the settlement, but certainly not enough for me to want him dead. Just some small sums, relating to the wholesale supply of olive oil, for his personal use. He claimed that the last consignment was rancid and refused to settle up with me."

"Was it actually rancid, by any chance?" Marcus interjected.

"Come, soldier," was the merchant's terse reply, "It depends on what your definition of rancid means. All I know is that I put a great deal of effort into purchasing the amphora and the scribe refused to pay for it. As to the olive oil's freshness, I cannot pass an opinion on it. Versillius, you know how difficult it is to obtain such goods at the present time…"

The centurion didn't answer and leaving Vespasianus to ponder on their questions, he walked out of his rooms into the market place. He was followed closely by Marcus, who asked him, "Do you actually think that he had any involvement, in the scribe's murder?"

"I can't be sure," Versillius replied, "He's one of the richest men in the town, but like all of us, perhaps a little bit short of money, now. You must have heard what he was saying to the market trader, when we approached him. And as well as the disagreement over licences, Antonius also owed him money. We already know that the scribe was also behind with his loan repayments to Paribius."

"But nobody seems to be involved in the revival of Mithras, other than Trajanius," Marcus countered.

"Well, so far no one had admitted it, other than our favourite legionnaire. But we do have three men closeting themselves away in a large villa. We also have the self styled leader of the cult suffering from a bad case of the runs. And for good measure we have an irate priestess, whom I would not care to wield a gladius against..."

As the younger man nodded his agreement, a faint voice from behind them said, "Excuse me for troubling you, gentlemen. I'm sure that you're both very busy...but I'd be very grateful if I could have a quiet word with you both?"

Versillius looked around and saw Partimius, junior scribe to the late Antonius. Despite being the dead man's junior, he was possibly the only person in Virulanium who might have a good word to say about him.

Chapter Ten

Partimius was a diffident, shy man of some thirty years of age and average height. He had worked with the scribe for over ten years and had always leapt to his defence, when others had complained about him. Although, to best of the centurion's knowledge, the two could not strictly have been descried as friends. Antonius was far too much of a stickler for the authority of his office, to socialise outside of work with his junior. But welcoming the junior scribe's approach, which he hoped might throw some light on the murder, Versillius asked, "Do you have some information for us?"

Partimius apprehensively, glanced around, looking at the crowd in the market place, as an anxious expression flickered across his face. Then he said, very nervously, "Well, I think I do...but not here. Follow me, please. It's much quieter and better, if we were to talk in the office..."

Partimius set off quickly towards the *principae,* or civic buildings, which were located inside the fort, on the western wall. Such was his speed of movement, that the two soldiers trailed in his wake, as they left both the fountain and temple behind them. It was obvious to Versillius and Marcus, that he did not wish to be seen talking to them in public. After crossing the western forum, they entered the fort, through the southern gate. The junior scribe maintained his swift pace, until they reached the principae. Like the settlement's temple, a portico fronted the administration's buildings. The structure was built in the style of a *basilica*, and topped with red pantiles to keep out the rain. When they arrived, he took them through the plastered entrance hall and down a side corridor, into a large office. As they looked for somewhere to sit down, Partimius said to them, "Thank you for your forbearance, officers. It really is most good of you to take the time to see me. I'm sorry about dragging you all the way here, but I need to talk to you in absolute privacy. In case you didn't know, this is poor Antonius' office. Mine is over there, towards the rear of this room. Of course, it is not so large or well appointed as..."

"I don't want to sound rude, but please get to the point, man! We don't have all day," Versillius said, somewhat abruptly, his patience beginning to wear thin after his late night and very trying morning.

"Forgive me, please...Antonius often chastised me about my tendency to ramble. He was right about that...and a lot of other things as well. I shall miss him you know." The junior scribe's voice tailed off, as he shook his head and bit his lip. Both Marcus and Versillius could see that he was very upset. So the centurion decided to take a softer approach and said to him, in a much lower voice, "I'm sorry for snapping at you, Partimius, but this is a very difficult time for us all. I understand your sorrow about these sad events and it is my intention to find out who was responsible. But to do that I need your help. Now, what was it that you wanted to tell us?"

Before answering, Partimius scurried over to his own office and peered into it, as if he was afraid of the presence of unknown intruders. He then walked all the way back, to the main door, and having made sure that it was closed firmly said, "This door was unlocked, when I arrived in the morning. I've never known Antonius leave the building without making sure that the office was secure. We have important papers in here, some of them come from as far away as Deva and *Londinium*. At one time they were sent all the way from Rome."

Versillius could see from his expression that Marcus was less than impressed by this revelation. But he immediately saw the significance of such a meticulous and pedantic man as Antonius leaving the office unlocked. So he replied, "What time did you leave here, last night?"

"As always, just after the sun set...my wife doesn't like me to be home too late. She is of a rather delicate disposition, what with two young children to look after. It's quite a strain on her you know..." Partimius halted in mid flow, realising that the centurion's expression had reverted to his angrier mode. He swallowed and resumed, " It was at my normal time to leave that Antonius told me that I was free to go home. He intended to stay on in the office, for a while, and deal with some high status correspondence. There had been a late delivery of letters from the governor and prefect, not to mention a communication from the legate. That was hand delivered by a messenger from *Banna*."

"Did you get to see these documents?" Marcus asked.

"No, but Antonius was reading them, as I left the office. And I don't suppose that I'll get to see them now. They are gone from his desk. That was the other thing that I meant to tell you."

Versillius then recalled that when examining the dead scribe's body that his keys, along with his purse and intaglio ring had been missing. Turning to Marcus he said, "I am sure that Antonius did not leave this office unlocked last night. Remember whoever killed him also stole the keys from his belt, as well as his intaglio ring and purse. Then his murderer came here and rifled the office. But then forgot to lock the door when the job was finished."

"Oh, goodness me!" Partimius said, "I had heard the talk in the forum that his purse and intaglio ring were missing. But his keys, as well as the correspondence from the governor and other important people..."

"Have any other documents disappeared?" the centurion cut in, wanting to finish this interview before the moon rose.

"I don't know, right now. He did tend to keep the most important communications to himself. But if you like, I'll be happy to search his desk and cabinet. It may be that I can find some empty or incomplete files."

"Please, go ahead," Versillius replied, "But if you do not know what papers you are looking for, then it will be a difficult task. I suggest that you look for the files relating to our senior officials and anything that may have been recently passed on from our trading community."

"The traders..." was the junior scribe's measured response, "I do know that they were displeased with the tax and licence fee increases. Just like the priestess was. But you must understand that Antonius was only carrying out the prefect's instructions. Now that the flow of money from Rome has dried up, we were told to maximise the town's revenues, for the health of the treasury. It was exactly the same with your reduced pay. Neither of us took any pleasure in holding money back from you." As the junior scribe finished, Marcus asked him, "What do you know about his dealings with Trajanius and the worship of Mithras?"

Partimius grimaced and replied, "Antonius decided that he couldn't confiscate the temple's assets without taking action against Trajanius. He wanted your legionnaire to pay a tax for worshipping a proscribed religion. Trajanius refused, saying that there was somebody involved who was very important. He said that Antonius would be in great trouble, if he took any action. It looks as if he was right..."

The room fell silent, as both Marcus and Versillius considered the man's words. The centurion was sure that Partimius had taken no enjoyment from levying the taxes, or withholding the back pay, but he was less sure about Antonius' motives. As he considered the implications, the junior scribe said, "But having told you what I know, I must now ask for your help. As you were no doubt aware, the scribe had no family. I suppose it is down to me to make sure he gets a proper funeral. Despite the weather, I've already made arrangements for a pyre to be built. Will you release the body and help me carry it to the cemetery? I'd do it on myself, but frankly, I'm not strong enough to manage the job on my own."

Partimius managed a nervous, half smile as he wrung his hands. The centurion put both the issues of the missing documents and the rifling of the office to one side. Antonius' junior was right. A man had died and he needed to be given the proper funerary rights. And if that involved Marcus and himself lending a hand, in the absence of anybody else, the so be it. The investigation could wait for a couple of hours. "Come with us," he said, "We'll return to the barracks and take his body to the funeral pyre for you. If we use enough animal fat, and dry brushwood, it will get the wood burning."

On the way back to the barracks, Versillius was full of remorse and self-doubt. His investigation was going nowhere, because apart from the traders, the priestess and Partimius' vague hints, he had no leads whatsoever. To the centurion's mind, his retirement could not come too soon. In his all career, he could not remember being so slipshod and under prepared in pursuing a murder investigation. He was determined to find out who had killed Antonius and why he had been murdered. But he realised that he had to somehow pull himself together and put together the strands of evidence that had already been gathered. As they approached the side room, where the body was stored, Versillius made a mental vow to resolve the murder. He also promised himself to conduct his enquiries in a more professional and logical manner. After almost twenty-five years of service, the centurion was not prepared to leave the army with a blemish on his record.

Two hours later, as the sun was starting to dip in the sky, the three men were stood in front of Antonius' last resting place. The Roman cemetery, which also served as a cremation area, was sited several hundred yards away from the fort's walls, in the northern part of the western vicus. It was only a short distance from the wooden Christian church, which had its own burial ground. Followers of their creed preferred interment in the soil, to long standing Roman tradition of cremation. Although some Roman families, who followed the pagan religion, were now opting for burials, rather than cremation. Fortunately for the three men, the rain held off for a while. With the help of animal fat and dry kindling, and much effort on the part of the legionnaires, the wooden pyre eventually caught light.

Because Antonius had not been religious, neither the priestess nor the Christian priest were required to officiate. It was left to Partimius to say some words, while the flames were fanned by the two soldiers and started to crawl up the tall, wooden structure. He started by wishing his dead colleague well in the after life. The junior scribe then went onto pray that the fire would cleanse the chief scribe's spirit and grant it a swift release from his body. For once, he didn't dither and both the other men could see from his features, that the sentiments were sincere and heartfelt. As he finished the brief eulogy, the centurion could see the tears in the man's eyes.

Versillius shuddered, because it seemed to him to be a sad end to a human being's life. As a soldier he was used to encountering death in its many forms. Although it was not the manner of Antonius' passing that perturbed him, but the paucity of his funeral rites. There were only three mourners present, of which two were legionnaires who had never had any time for him. The other was his subordinate from work, whom he had steadfastly refused to socialise with, due to the man's inferior status. It was said that the scribe had even insisted that they visit the communal lavatories and baths at different times. Being an unmarried man and without children, the centurion could quite easily see himself being despatched in a similar fashion. Of course this was something that he hoped was more than a few years down the road. But it was an unedifying and bleak prospect. Feeling chastened and saddened, he placed a consoling arm around Partimius before saying to him, "The flames will take some time to do their work. I think we should return to the fort now, as it is starting to get late. You can collect and bury the ashes in an urn tomorrow, when the fire has burnt itself out. And if this funeral in any way puts you out of pocket, I will personally ensure that the administration reimburses you."

"That will not be necessary," the junior scribe replied, "Antonius may not considered me to have been a friend, but I thought of myself as his friend. I respected and liked him, both as a man and a colleague...even if he never invited me to his villa and refused to bathe with me. He was my superior and that was his decision."

"And you must not reproach yourself, in any way whatsoever," Versillius added, "Lesser men would have left his body to rot in my care. I salute and respect you for caring enough to see that the proper rites were observed."

Partimius seemed to take some solace from the centurion's words. After a few moments he said, "Thank you for your kind words, centurion. But you also spoke the truth about us needing to depart. I've got those files of his to inspect before the sun falls. After what happened to Antonius, I don't want my wife to start worrying about me, if I'm late home."

Although before they could leave the cremation, a figure in a roughly, woven brown robe approached the funeral party. It was brother Paulus the Christian priest. When he reached the pyre, he said, "I saw the flames and smoke rising, from the outside of my wooden church. Would you like me to give the departed soul a blessing?"

Partimius explained that the chief scribe was a non believer, but that such an action could do no harm. Paulus made the sign of the cross and clasped his hands in prayer, saying, "Antonius, may your lord, whoever he is, receive your soul and take it unto his bosom. Whether it is my Christian heaven or the Roman underworld, then God speed." Turning to the three other men he said, "See, true to my faith, I bear ill will to no man. Even to the scribe who had threatened to increase the taxes that my impoverished church pays! A man who asserted that our Lord Jesus Christ had never existed. And what use is his cleverness and learning to him now? But I bear him no malice and tonight I will pray again for his tormented soul..."

Yet another potential suspect, Versillius thought to himself, as they departed and left the flames to do their work.

Chapter Eleven

The junior scribe seemed to recover some of his composure, as they walked along the *via* west and returned to the fort. He promised to examine Antonius' personal files, in great detail, and report any suspicions about missing documents on the following day. As they watched him walk into the civic offices, Marcus asked, "Just a thought sir, but do you think that the scribe could have taken the missing correspondence to his villa? It is possible that he intended to deal with it overnight?"

"I doubt it," Versillius responded, "According to Partimius, he remained in the office until late. Remember, the sun had fallen before his assistant departed. He stayed on specifically to deal with communications, which he did not want the junior man to see. He may not even have returned to his villa last night. And why would anyone want to steal his keys and enter the offices, unless they were sure that the documents were still there?"

"You are probably correct, centurion. But his domestic keys were also a part of the missing bundle. So if you have no objection, I'll visit his home and make a quick check of the premises. Maybe, I could find something there that might help our enquiry, even if it is just another unlocked door."

"A good point, go and see what you can find. While you do that, I need to have a quick word with Artemis. Until Partimius, who may have widened the net, approached us the doctor was the last man on my own list of suspects to interview. By his own admission, he was constantly disagreeing with Antonius. They nearly came to blows on one more than one occasion, when the scribe denounced him as a charlatan."

"I remember it very well, sir. The two of them were arguing in the forum and had to be separated, by your merchant friends. Didn't they also pull you away from Antonius, when you had your dispute about the ballista and modern day training methods for new recruits?"

Versillius halted and thought to himself that his junior needed to learn some lessons in diplomacy, before replying, "A professional reputation is very important to a doctor, Marcus. A lot more important than that of a hot headed centurion. Besides, Artemis would also have been subject to the same threat of tax and rent increases as my friends the traders. The administration would view medicine as a taxable profession. Meet me in the tavern, when you finish at the scribe's villa."

Marcus nodded in agreement, but slightly reticently, as he was not a great drinker himself. Versillius set off for the doctor's surgery, pondering the best way to pursue the lead that the junior scribe had given him. Missing correspondence from the prefect, the governor and the legate. Such a line of investigation was not going to be easy to follow. Their rank and seniority was almost enough to put him off. But the killing of a man was a crime in any circumstances and it was his job to solve it. No matter who was involved or how important they were. However, he realised that given the importance of their positions, his enquiries would have to be tactful. Otherwise his pension, and hoped for comfortable retirement, would be put at risk.

Leaving the fort by the southern gate, he entered the vicus, crossed the western forum and reached the offices, where Artemis maintained his practice. The physician was sat in his surgery, studying some notes. As it was late in the afternoon, most of his patients had been treated already, so the centurion only had a short time to wait in the ante chamber. When Versillius walked into the consulting room, the grey haired, wiry physician looked up from his reading. He glanced at the centurion, and like the other suspects, said without any enthusiasm, "So it's my turn to be questioned, is it? I take it that you must have finished with the market traders."

"You have your job to do and I have mine, Artemis. I'll try to keep this as brief as possible, where were you last night?"

"In my villa, where you and your handsome young soldier found me, after your visit to the prefect. I'd been there all night reading a treatise from Greece, on the best use of herbs and honey, in treating flesh wounds. You might find the knowledge that I gained useful, one day," the physician replied.

"I sincerely hope that such treatment will not be necessary, in my case. But I must say, Artemis, that you didn't seem in the slightest bit sorry or surprised to find out about the murder of Antonius, last night."

"My only surprise was that it hadn't happened sooner, as the man had it coming to him. That is in my professional opinion, speaking as the community's doctor and soothsayer," he answered, with just the slightest hint of a smile on his face.

The centurion paused briefly, noting the physician's grin, before saying, "Would this have anything to do with your disagreements in various public places? Or maybe, it could be related to his demands to increase the cost of your licence to practice medicine in Virulanium? And there is also the matter of the rent increase for your premises to be considered, as well."

"Of course not!" the physician shouted, his grin totally gone, "I just didn't like the fellow. Nobody did, as I am sure that you have already been told. But that surely doesn't mean that I killed him? You might as well arrest everybody in Virulanium, yourself included!"

"Calm down, Artemis, these are only routine questions, that have to be asked."

"I'll try and remember that, the next time you suffer from an ailment and come to me for treatment," he replied, huffily.

"Don't threaten me, doctor, I'm just trying to remove you from the enquiry, rather than have you arrested. I don't suppose you have a witness to back up your whereabouts at the time of the murder?"

"Well, no," the physician answered, "As a single man, I live on my own. I don't even have a slave to vouch for me."

"Not that their testimony would be admitted to a court of law," Versillius answered, "But for what it's worth, I believe your testimony and am truly sorry for taking up your time."

The doctor was less than impressed and grunted back at him, "It is my job to save lives, rather than end one. Even when that life belongs to an obnoxious, little turd like Antonius. Tell me centurion, why are you Romans so damned arrogant? Every civilising influence you posses come from Greece; philosophy, drama, medicine and even your old religion. You Romans stole them all from us. Then along comes a man like your chief scribe, who claims to know more about my country's contribution than I, a native born Greek!"

Having finished speaking, he bowed his head and returned to his notes and Versillius left his surgery. Despite his closing diatribe, the centurion was still prepared to accept the physician's word. This was mainly due to the man's age and height. He was much older and smaller than the dead scribe. As far as Versillius was aware, he had never wielded a sword in his life. It was almost impossible for him to have struck the fatal blow. Artemis had also been fast asleep in his bed, when the two legionnaires had disturbed him, the previous night. The centurion's final reason for believing him was that the worship of Mithras had never appealed to the Greeks. Because of their long standing enmity and dislike of the Persians, Greek people had ignored Mithraism, at the time when Romans were enthusiastically embracing it. That fact alone was enough to rule out the physician. Of course, the Greeks were never short of deities to worship, even if Rome had appropriated and renamed their gods. Versillius was still unsure as to how exactly the cult of Mithras was involved in the murder of Antonius. But his instincts told him that it was.

  The centurion then walked towards the south gate, but headed in the direction of the tavern, rather than back to the fort. After the day's interrogations, he was feeling in great need of a draught or two, of Caracalla's cloudy beer. But his progress was interrupted by the sound of imperial trumpets from outside the east gate. Their loud blasts could mean only one thing; the twentieth legion's legate, Appius Severus, had finally decided to visit Virulanium. Which bearing in mind the missing correspondence from the chief scribe's office, the centurion found very interesting. It also meant that there was no danger whatsoever of an attack by the Picts. Versillius had served under the same commanding officer for many years and held him in complete and utter contempt. This was because he had long considered Appius Severus to be the only non-combatant to reach such a high rank in the imperial army. As a political appointee, the man had never faced the spears or swords of an enemy in battle. Although this did not stop him from sending his own legionnaires northwards, to face the dangers that he had always avoided. So much for the twentieth legion's title: *Valeria Victrix,* the Victorious Eagle.

Chapter Twelve

Ignoring the arrival of the legate and his party, Versillius slipped past the southern gate, not noticed by the sentry. The man's attention was obviously distracted by the arrival of such high ranking visitors. He continued on his way to Caracalla's tavern. The bar was a white plaster walled building, which had supporting wooden beams. These were inset into the exterior walls and the tavern also had a wooden balcony at its front. After entering the premises, the centurion sat in his usual place. He realised that the hour was early, as far as drinking alcohol was concerned. But he was still pleased when the proprietor, Caracalla placed a clay beaker of ale in front of him. The tavern's owner was an ex-legionnaire, in his late fifties and a former comrade, of both himself and Marcus' father. A short, thick set man, similar in build to the centurion, he had taken his retirement over ten years ago and invested his pension in the business. As the centurion reached for the drink, Caracalla said, "I imagine that you've had quite a hard day, if the talk in the forum is to be believed. Believe me, old friend, you are not too popular in this settlement. A person might think that you had personally killed the dead man."

Versillius nodded and before picking up his drink, replied, "You can believe the gossip. I've annoyed so many fellow citizens today that I'm almost afraid to visit the communal lavatories tomorrow morning. Perhaps I'll walk down to the river and unload myself there, alongside the thatched house dwellers and native Britons."

The bar owner smiled at his comments, as the centurion drained his cup and then asked for a refill.

While his beaker was being replenished, Marcus returned from the dead man's villa. Versillius gestured for a second to be brought and after waiting for Caracalla to move away, asked, "Did you find anything at the scribe's home?"

The young man shook his head and replied, "The front door was locked and there were no signs of a break in. I went around to the back door and found that was also locked too. Failing all else I approached his nearest neighbour, who claims that the scribe did not return to his residence last night. The man had a spare key for the front door, which he was kind enough to give me..."

"That is so typical of Antonius," Versillius interjected, "I'll wager that he'd have worn two belts around his trousers, if it wasn't so uncomfortable."

Marcus chuckled at that and continued, "I searched the main rooms and could find nothing to do with his official business. There were numerous scrolls and layers of papyrus, as well as some sheets of parchment that he had written upon himself. They were all mainly to do with medical matters. But there was not a thing that you could relate back to the business of the civic administration."

That was just what the centurion had expected the soldier to find. Seeing his subordinate toying with his beer, he said, "Marcus, are you going to drink that or just look at it?"

The younger soldier answered, "I'm by no means a great lover of the beer, sir. I mean no offence, but perhaps you would care to down it for me? Of course, I'll pay for the next round."

Versillius glanced down at his own cup, which seemed to be almost empty and decided to take the legionnaire up on his offer. While the centurion was draining the dregs from his own beaker, the young man said, "I heard the trumpet sounds on my way here, from the western side of the vicus. Does that mean that the general is now in our midst?"

"Unfortunately so, I'm afraid. And it may have something to do with the murder of the scribe. Our less than beloved, commanding officer very rarely ventures this far east, along the Wall – it might be too dangerous for him. I dare say that we, or I, will be summoned to his presence in the morning. But until that happens, I am definitely going to keep a low profile."

Marcus suddenly looked very awkward and said, "I'm very sorry sir, but can I be excused? Please don't take this personally, but I must go back to the barracks and eat something. Other than our snack, in the forum, I haven't eaten all day. The cooks will be about to serve our evening meal."

Unlike his thirst, Versillius had never had a big appetite for food, at the best of times. He gave the younger man permission to depart. Marcus dropped two silver coins on the table and set off, to return to the barracks. As the centurion sat alone, watching the sun finally dip beneath the cloudy horizon, he briefly contemplated the murder case. He was starting to feel more confident in his handling of the enquiry, mainly because of the work that had been completed. The investigation had started with six possible suspects, all of whom had been interviewed. Which was not a bad day's work in itself. But since talking to Partimius the list had grown to nine. On the minus side, he had already realised that the next stage was not going to be easy to resolve. On the plus side, he was pleased with the way that Marcus had carried himself so far. The young man seemed to know when to ask the suspects questions or when to remain silent, in the background. Then after he had drunk two more beers, Versillius was glad to see that it was getting dark outside. This was just what he had been waiting for. After the sad thoughts that had occurred to him at the scribe's funeral, it was time for the centurion to visit the house of pleasure.

Caracalla saw that he was about to leave and walked across to his table. The bar owner was able to speak freely, as there were no other customers present. As Versillius rose to his feet, the former legionnaire said, "Listen to me, centurion. You need to watch your back. I bumped into that idiot Trajanius, earlier. All joking apart, he has got it in for you, in a big way. He told me that last night, not only had you insulted Mithras, but you had also personally humiliated him."

"I did no more than he deserved, Caracalla, and far less than I could have done. In your day, a legionnaire would never have left his post to visit the lavatorium, would he?"

"Not without getting a severe beating, from the centurion or his comrades. Just be careful, Versillius. Not only do I like you, but also your custom keeps my head above water. And before you ask, I rebuffed Trajanius several months ago, when he asked me to join the cult of Mithras. I never embraced it twenty years ago, when Marcus Pontius' father was running things. Why should I get involved now? Just because I was once a soldier, it doesn't mean that he can tell me what to do."

Outside, in the cool early evening air, Versillius was pleased that the tavern owner has warned him about his incorrigible legionnaire. One part of him wanted to storm back to the barracks and confront Trajanius. But at the same time, he realised that was the wrong thing to do. It was a far better strategy to allow the man to pay out enough rope to ensnare himself. Let Trajanius walk around the vicus, shooting his mouth off. Versillius knew that he still had enough friends for the comments to get back to him. And when the centurion was sure of his grounds, he would strike, swiftly and hard. Even if a pater of the highest level of devotion protected Trajanius, they would do him little or no good. But for now he had other business to attend to, before the hour grew too late.

Chapter Thirteen

The house of pleasure was located close to the tavern, on the eastern side of the fort's outside wall. A plain façade fronted a single floored building, which had ten rooms or chambers, where the prostitutes entertained their clients. It had been a constant source of great surprises for Versillius, when he was a naïve, young legionnaire. Not the least of these had been to find out that not all the establishment's customers were men. He had also been amazed to discover that not all of the workers were female, although that practice seemed to have fallen by the wayside in recent times. Within the individual rooms were solid stone slabs, which were covered in hay and animal skins, to make them slightly more comfortable. Above each door was a pornographic image of what a man or woman might expect to experience inside, a picture of each prostitute's speciality.

The working women effectively rented the rooms from the brothel's owner, Flavala. As he had assured Gaius Flavius, the previous night, there still was quite a high turnover of personnel. Once a prostitute had earned enough money, to pay off a debt or buy a house, she might retire. That was unless she enjoyed her work, something which was not unknown in many parts of the empire. But whenever retirements occurred, Versillius had never noticed a shortage of new women ready to take their place. Not all were from the settlement. Because of the popularity of Virulanium, Flavala's recruits came from far and wide. In that respect, her establishment greatly resembled the legion that it serviced.

As he entered the vestibule, the proprietor approached him and said, "It may be already dark, but you are early tonight, centurion. I'm afraid that your favourite girl is not here yet. Perhaps her husband has not yet fallen asleep."

He smiled at Flavala, who was an attractive, auburn haired woman, some five years younger than he was. She was wearing a cream full-length tunica, which was belted at the waist and below her bust. Around her shoulders, she had thrown a blue *palla* or female's cloak, as protection against the cold. Versillius remembered very well her younger days, when she had still been a working girl. In those days he had enjoyed her services many times. At the time, just like the soldier, she had been starting out on her chosen profession. But unlike many of the women from that era, she had saved her money. With the help of a loan from Paribius, Flavala had eventually ended up as the sole owner of the brothel and had become a good business woman in addition.

"Flavala," he replied, "I'm not here for my favourite girl, as you call her. Tonight, I want to talk to you."

"Or do you mean that you want to interrogate me? Am I also suspected of the murder of Antonius, now?" she answered, her feisty temper showing.

"Not at all. Look, I came here early tonight because I need to see you – and to see you alone. Can we go somewhere more private and spend some time together, please?"

Flavala looked at him and said, with a confused expression on her face, "Other than yourself, there are no clients here at the moment. If you really want to talk to me, I suppose we could go to my private rooms. That might even bring back some memories for you, centurion! Although, you must remember that I am no longer in the business of selling myself to legionnaires for a few coins."

"It will bring back more than a few memories, of more than a few of my coins. I seem to recall spending most of my wages on you, some years ago," he said, in reply.

She smiled at his response and suddenly looked almost ten years younger. For the first time since he had entered the building, Flavala seemed to relax. With the atmosphere between them lightened, they walked together towards the rear of the building. Versillius found his eyes uncontrollably looking upwards, as they passed the frescos that depicted almost every imaginable sexual act. They had been freshly repainted, in lurid, bright colours, since his last visit a few days earlier and were more lucid than ever. Inside her apartment, Flavala sat him down and disappeared briefly. The centurion glanced down at the plain, tiled floor and then up at the tastefully painted plaster walls. In a moment, she returned, with two glasses of with red wine. Handing him one, she said, "Now there's something special for you. We have precious little red wine left in our settlement. But as one of my oldest and best customers, I think you deserve it. Although, I shudder to think, Versillius, that if I ever lose your custom what it will do to my business's turnover."

"Caracalla told me the same thing, not ten minutes ago," he replied, "It seems that my legacy to Virulanium will have been to ensure that the two most disreputable establishments stayed in business." Versillius then took the green glass and raised it to the light, before sipping at the liquid. It was stale, but still tasted good, a welcome relief from the cloudy, brown ale that the tavern served. Flavala watched as he savoured each mouthful, before asking him,

"So what exactly do you want to talk to me about, if it's not the death of our poor and unlamented scribe?"

"Well it is about the death of Antonius, but only in an indirect way..."

Her face bristled at his comment, thinking that she was under suspicion, but he quickly continued, "I was at his cremation today. Just myself, Marcus and his subordinate Partimius. Only three people present and not one that he would have even remotely considered to be a friend. There wasn't even a relative in sight. It struck me as a very sad way for a man to be despatched to the underworld, if there is such a thing awaiting us."

"So what does that have to do with me?" she countered, looking confused at his words and reasoning. This was not the Versillius that she had known for over twenty years, talking. Especially as he suddenly paused, as if the words in his mind were unable to travel the short distance to his mouth. Eventually, he rose to his feet and managed to say, "Flavala...neither you or I have any family. And neither of us has ever been married. I'm about to complete my twenty-five years of service and have purchased a villa. It might not be in the better part of the western vicus, but I'm sure that you will like it. When I leave the army, there'll be a pension and...and..." It was at that point that the centurion completely lost the thread of what he had intended to say. He awkwardly wrung his hands together, as the ability to speak cogently deserted him completely.

Flavala, suddenly burst out laughing and putting the soldier out of his misery said, "Are you trying to make some sort of a proposal to me, Versillius? A centurion in the imperial army asking for the hand of a former working girl? Not to mention the current owner of the settlement's only house of pleasure."

He bit his lip, nodded and replied, "Flavala, our past has gone now and in more ways than one. But I believe that we are both still young enough to have something of a future together. Whatever happens to either Virulanium, or the empire in the years ahead, I think it would be better if we faced it together. These thoughts have been on my mind for some time, but attending the cremation of Antonius put it all into perspective. That is why I am standing here now, gibbering like an imbecile."

She looked him directly in the eyes and said, "Versillius, I believe that you are being serious and honest with me. But I need some time to think your proposal over, before I can give you my answer. What you have just told me, has come as a something of a shock. I'm sure that you understand what I'm trying to say, don't you?"

"I do, Flavala and apologise for not putting my feelings more clearly. It's just that I'm not used to expressing myself, in such a way..."

"Versillius, you have no need to apologise," Flavala replied, "In fact, I suppose I should feel quite flattered. But in the meantime, it would help my considerations greatly if you stopped being one of my best customers. After all, I'm still a woman, as well as being the owner of this most disreputable establishment."

He bowed his head, in acknowledgement of her request. She then went onto say to him, "Actually, centurion, I had meant to speak with you this night. But not about anything so personal as a proposal. Whether this will help you or not I don't know, but your dead scribe was also one of my good customers. The only difference between yourself and Antonius, was that he usually came here very discretely and always through the rear entrance. He told me that his high office in the administration meant that he could not afford to be seen visiting my premises. Just like the prefect, who is so terrified that his wife will find out about his visits."

"And was the scribe here last night?"

"Oh, yes! That is exactly what I wanted to tell you. He came straight from the civic offices and stayed until late, enjoying himself with two of my girls," she replied.

"Two girls?" the centurion asked, as the late scribe suddenly went up in his estimation. Versillius was now more than pleased. Despite not getting an answer to his proposal from Flavala, he had obtained another piece of the puzzle relating to the death of Antonius. This was the reason that the scribe had been outside the domestic comfort of his villa, so late at night. He had been seeking pleasures of a more carnal nature than his dry texts could offer. From there, it was only a small leap of the imagination to imagine that somebody must have followed him from the civic building. Then, after waiting for him to emerge from to the brothel, he could easily have been followed through the forum by his assailant and murdered. "I thank you for that," he said, "But for my sake, please do not think for too long on my suggestion. I know it would work well for us both. To me you are still the same young, auburn haired minx that I first encountered in this establishment twenty years ago..."

"Go back to the barracks and sleep, Versillius. You lost the ability to charm me with your tongue, many years ago. Do you think that I've forgotten how you dropped me and started visiting the younger girls who worked here? And that was some years before I even bought this place. But I promise that you'll have my answer within the week."

Putting on a brave face, the centurion grinned and drained the last few drops from his glass, before bidding her a good night. Flavala noted his deflated demeanour and smiled inwardly to herself, as she gently squeezed her moist thighs together. Despite his attentions to her younger prostitutes, she had never been able to lose her affection or feelings for him. But she was in no mood to appear too much of a pushover. So as he walked down the corridor, instead of pushing him into one of the chambers and jumping on top of the soldier, she shouted, "And you'll also need to spend a lot less time in Caracalla's bar, than you usually do. That is, if you want to get a favourable reply from me!"

Taking her words at face value, he just about managed summon up the willpower to walk past the tavern door. This was particularly hard because the building was sited directly at the side of the southern gate. But he returned straight to the barracks – despite the relatively early hour, because his intentions towards Flavala were heartfelt.

Chapter Fourteen

Unlike his men, who shared the legionary dormitories between them, the centurion had a substantial set of rooms for his own private use. Most native Britons would have considered his suite to be a high status home, in its own right. This was because the fort's living quarters had originally been built to station over two hundred soldiers. At a pinch and with the use of pitched tents, they could house a whole cohort for a month, or longer. But the empire's constant troop withdrawals to the continent had depleted the forces stationed along the Northern frontier. Now, the fort had only eighty men living there and more than enough living space to share around. Versillius had not been back in his chambers for very long and was stretched out on his bed, when he heard a knock on the wooden entrance door. As he was still wearing his red tunica, he rose from his half slumber, and walked through several rooms, before shouting, after the manner of the prefect, "Who in the name of Hades is that? I'm trying to get some much needed rest after a very busy day!"

"It's Marcus," a voice replied, "I'm sorry to disturb you, but we have company, sir. It's Getilla, Partimius' wife."

The centurion wondered what she was doing in the barracks at such a late hour. He opened the door to find out and his two visitors walked in. Getilla was a plump, raven haired woman in her late twenties. She had been married to the junior scribe for over fifteen years and they had two young children. Versillius knew that something serious must have happened, because there were tears in her reddened eyes and her forehead was creased with worry lines. Her normally pleasant and affable manner had been replaced with one of anxiety and nervous agitation. Marcus placed a steadying hand on her shoulder and started to explain, on her behalf, "Getilla came to the barracks, sir, because her husband has not yet returned home. She was starting to feel very concerned for his safety. Especially, after the events of the previous night."

Versillius gestured for her to sit down, noting that her legs seemed somewhat unsteady.

"What he says is true, centurion" Getilla added, as she gratefully took the weight of her feet, "Almost every night for the past ten years, my husband has returned to our home, just as the sun goes down. His routine almost never varies, unless Antonius requires him to stay late. But as the chief scribe is now dead that could not have happened tonight. After waiting for some time, I left our home and looked for him around the forum. I even went into the tavern, which he never visited, just to be sure. But there was no sign of him to be found..."

"Did you try the civic buildings, Getilla? Partimius may have fallen asleep at his desk. He told me that he was going to be working a little late on some of the administration's files, to help us with our investigation," Versillius asked her.

"Yes, I did go there, centurion. But the buildings were securely locked up and there was no sign of any light from their interior. After that, I didn't know what else to do, other than to come to the barracks for help. I just can't stop worrying and remembering about what happened to poor Antonius, last night."

Versillius could understand her concern. Thinking swiftly, he said, "We have a duplicate set of master keys to the civic buildings, in the guard room. I will go there with Marcus and see what we can find.

But I want you to return to your home and tend to your children. We'll come to see you, as soon as we have any news." He then left his chambers, and called for a member of the watch. When the soldier arrived, Versillius asked him to escort Getilla safely to her house, which was situated in the western vicus. The centurion's firm tone and purpose seemed to slightly reassure the distraught woman. She departed, after thanking Versillius for his efforts, in the company of the soldier. While he was making the arrangement, Marcus had gone to the guardroom, to find the spare set of master keys. He returned within a few minutes, and the two men left the barracks, walking into the cold night air. Both men wrapped their brown paenula cloaks tightly around their bodies. On the way to the civic offices, Versillius said, "I don't know what's happening in Virulanium at the moment. Two scribes; one dead and one missing, in just a single day, it totally beggars belief!"

    His subordinate could only agree with him, as they completed the short walk to the western side of the fort. The two men saw that the buildings were in total darkness, exactly as Getilla had described them to be. Fortunately, Marcus had taken a lighted torch from the barracks, so at least they were able to see their way. Using the spare set of master keys, Versillius unlocked the heavy, main door and let them into the entrance hall. Unable to detect any sign of life, or otherwise, they went straight to the office that Partimius had taken them to earlier in the day. But after they had searched his room and all the other offices, the result was exactly the same as it had been in the entrance hall. Apart from themselves, there was nobody in the civic building, either dead or alive. It was then that an idea came to the centurion, he turned to Marcus, saying, "The cremation area!

Suppose Partimius went there, after finishing work on the files? Maybe he wanted to make one last farewell to Antonius, on his way home. That must be the answer, if he is nowhere else to be found."

"You could be right, sir, I noticed that he was very reluctant to leave the pyre this afternoon," the younger man replied.

It took them ten minutes to reach the cemetery. This was even though they had the set of master keys and were therefore able to use the western gate, which was securely locked for the night. From the fort's wall they could see that Antonius' pyre was still glowing brightly. Although as they approached the cremation area, by the via west, the centurion sensed that something was wrong. The wooden structure had not burnt down as much as it should have done. The explanation for this became clear, when they reached the funeral pyre. Both the soldiers quickly realised that it was no longer the chief scribe's funeral pyre alone. He was now sharing it with Partimius, who was lying face up on top of Antonius. In shock, Marcus dropped his torch and the two men rushed towards the fire. Moving upwind, because of the intense heat, they grabbed the junior scribe by his feet and hauled him off the flaming, hot wood. But their actions were to no great avail, as the man was obviously already dead. The back of his clothes had already started to smoulder, so they rolled his corpse in the soil, until the burning cloth was doused. Then Versillius examined him, in the light of the fire and found, to no great surprise a gladius sized wound in his stomach. "It looks as if our killer has struck again," he said to Marcus, who after examining the body, responded,

"The wound looks exactly the same, as the one that did for Antonius. It's even in the same part of the body. What do you think happened, sir?"

"It is as I suspected. He came to pay his final respects to Antonius and was killed here. Look, you can see traces of his blood on the grass, over there. They probably caught him off guard, while he was praying for the dead man. Partimius probably never realised that he was about to join his superior in the after world."

"They...you said "they", how do you know that there is more than one person involved in the killings?"

"Well, I personally couldn't lift this man and raise him onto a five foot funeral pyre, which already had one half burnt body on it. Just think of the difficulty that we had, lifting Antonius up there, this afternoon. There had to be more than one of them, to raise him that high."

Marcus had to agree with his logic. On the off chance of spotting something, that his superior might have missed, he looked closely at the body of Partimius. Using the glow from the fire, he checked first for the man's purse, after his error on the previous night. It was not on the dead man's belt, so he said, "Sir, it's a copycat killing, just like with the murder of Antonius. His purse is missing..."

"I'd spotted that already, as I examined his stomach wound," the centurion interjected.

"But I bet you didn't see the scrap of parchment that he has clenched in his right fist!" Marcus countered, with a tone of satisfaction in his voice. Versillius hadn't and quickly reached for the dead man's hand. Between them they prised it open and took out a small and badly charred piece of vellum. Holding it against the fire the two men could make out only one word; *solidus*. The centurion held the scrap higher and saw that it was all that was left of a torn corner piece. Turning to Marcus, he said, "He must have found something in the files. Now, did he bring the documents here to burn them, or did his killers murder him to snatch them from him?"

"Your guess is as good as any, sir. but what do you want me to do now?"

"Tell me that you noticed that his intaglio ring is also missing. Or am I teaching you nothing about murder investigations?" the older man asked.

"I'm learning, sir, I promise. It's just that you have done this before and I have not."

Versillius acknowledged his junior's words. But the centurion knew that the next step of the investigation was not going to be very pleasant, for either himself or Getilla. Marcus was detailed to return to the fort, and with the help of the guard move the second body back to the barracks. "We have no need to disturb the physician, on this occasion. I doubt that he can tell us any more than we already know," Versillius told the younger legionnaire, "If you take care of the body's removal, then I will go and talk to Partimius' widow. Somebody has to give her the sad news."

As Marcus departed, the centurion set off to inform Getilla about the loss of her husband. In his mind, he also pondered the wisdom of letting the prefect know about the junior scribe's murder before the morning. It would be even more awkward than usual to approach the easily irritated official, because he would be entertaining the legate and the governor. Wherever the general travelled along the Wall, then the governor Quintus Lucius was always found in his wake. The centurion was not that worried about the governor, who was usually a placid man to deal with. But the arrival of the legate had put him in an awkward position. In theory, as the fort's centurion, he should have presented himself to the legion's commanding officer, upon hearing the imperial trumpets. However, with his impending retirement and his view that the man was a complete fool, he had made a snap decision to lie low and keep out of the general's way. But he was still unsure of what exactly to do after his visit to Getilla, as he approached the dead scribe's thatched house.

Chapter Fifteen

Partimius had been unable to afford a villa, on the modest civic salary of a junior scribe. He had lived with his family in a thatched house, of medium status, on the far western side of the vicus. The wooden, plastered structures were smaller and cheaper to build or purchase than the stone walled, pantiled villas. Versillius thought that this might have been another reason why Antonius had never socialised with his subordinate. Not only was the man his junior at work, he had also lived in thatched accommodation. Many in the high status community considered such buildings, and their inhabitants, to be inferior to themselves and their own dwellings. Although such considerations had never concerned the centurion in the slightest bit. From what he had seen and known of Partimius, it was his opinion that the man had been a far better and more decent person, than a lot of his so called superiors, especially his immediate superior in the civic administration.

It was some minutes since he had arrived at the outside of the dead man's home. Versillius knew that he couldn't spend the whole night standing and shivering outside the plastered house. He realised that sooner, rather than later, he would have to break the sad news to Getilla. This was another part of his job that he didn't relish and looked forward to relinquishing. After swallowing heavily and finally plucking up his courage, he approached the entrance and knocked hard on the door, shouting, "Getilla, it's Versillius. We need to come talk, can I come in?"

She came to the door in a split second, opening it and pulling the heavy draft excluding curtain to the side, in one motion. But seeing that the centurion was on his own, Getilla immediately burst into tears. Versillius took hold of her hands and lead her into the main part of her home, saying, "I'm sorry - very, very sorry. But we found your husband's body in the cemetery. There was nothing that either I, or Marcus could do to help him. He was already dead when we arrived."

Getilla immediately pulled away from him. She refused to be comforted and replied, "I feared the worst, when he was so late in returning home. But tell me, how did my husband die?"

"There is no easy way to tell you this, but you have every right to know. Partimius went to the cremation area to say his last farewells to Antonius. Whoever killed him inflicted a stab wound to his stomach. They probably caught him unawares, at the side of Antonius' pyre." There was no reply. So he paused, to let the details sink in. Then he continued, "I imagine that he decided to pay his final respects, before returning home to you. On my instructions, Marcus is having his body removed to the barracks. I'll help you make the appropriate arrangements tomorrow. But I give you my solemn promise that I will track his murderers down and make sure that they face justice."

She shook her head from side to side and paced agitatedly around the fire, at the rear of the room. Then wringing her hands, Getilla eventually replied, "It just isn't fair! Please forgive me for saying this, centurion, but when I heard that Antonius was dead, I thought that our life would get better, not worse. After all his years of loyal service to the administration, I saw my husband becoming the chief scribe. And finally, our young family would be able to afford to live in a villa. But now that Partimius has been killed, it will never happen!"

"I have already promised to find out who his murderers are and ensure that they are punished. Of course, I'll do anything else in my power to help you and your family, through this difficult time."

"That isn't it," she yelled back at him, loudly, causing the children, who were sleeping in a rear room to stir, "You can not even begin to understand my position, Versillius. In a few months time, you will retire on a good pension, to a nice property on the eastern side of the vicus. What will have become of my family by then? Other than my husband, we now have no income and there is money that is still owed to Paribius, for the purchase of our home."

Versillius was momentarily lost for words, but was soon able to answer, "Listen, Getilla, I am unable to say too much, at the present time. But I have my suspicions. If they turn out to be justified then, I am sure that you will be compensated for your husband's loss. In the meantime, I will make good your repayments to Paribius and help your family, as best that I can...no strings attached. Getilla, I am very sorry, but I must go. It may be late, but I do have some more work to do..."

She glanced up at the centurion and appeared to recover some of her composure. Getilla even managed a faint smile and thanked him for the trouble that he had taken, before saying, "Please, make sure that you catch his killer and give me the satisfaction of seeing him suffer the same fate that my husband did. Forget the words that I said about living in a villa. It was just a dream that Partimius and I shared for many years and now it's gone. I also thank you kindly for your offer of financial assistance. But as I have children to attend to and tears to release, I bid you farewell,"

Versillius left the thatched house, as Getilla went to comfort her children, who had risen from their beds. He hadn't mentioned to her that they had found the body on the funeral pyre, as she was obviously upset enough. Like the legate and the prefect, that was a problem for the morning. But despite the late hour he had no intention of sleeping, yet. Instead, he walked through the western vicus and skirted the fort's walls. He was heading in the direction of Vespasianus' villa, which was on the eastern side of the settlement. The merchant had invited him to inspect his petition that night and after the second murder, the centurion had decided it was time to take him up on his offer.

Chapter Sixteen

It took him almost fifteen minutes to make the journey to the eastern vicus. But when he arrived, the centurion could see light shining from the windows of the merchant's home. At least he had not had a wasted journey. Walking up to the villa's front door, he knocked and waited. Vespasianus eventually answered, shouting, from behind the locked door, "Who's there?"

"It's Versillius, I need to talk to you, urgently."

The door opened slowly and slightly, as the merchant took his time to turn the key and release the bolts. He then held up his oil lamp and in its faint glow checked the centurion's identity, to his own satisfaction. The door opened wider and Vespasianus said to him, with more than a tone of exasperation in his voice, "Haven't you harassed me enough today?"

"There has been a another murder. Partimius, the junior scribe, was recently found dead in the cemetery. I'm actually here to try and clear your name, as well as take up your offer of inspecting the petition to the governor," Versillius responded. If Vespasianus was surprised at these words, he didn't show it. Although, he did hesitate slightly before saying,

"Well, in that case, I suppose that you'd better come through. We were just about to finish working on our submission to Quintus Lucius. At this very moment, Paribius and Domitius are writing the last words. We've been hard at it all night." He led the legionnaire into a large side room, where his fellow traders were poring over a stack of parchment and a table full of scrolls. Vespasianus said to them, "Our centurion tells me that there has been another killing.

This time it has been the settlement's junior scribe. Perhaps you might care to stop drafting our petition, Paribius, while he asks us some questions? And try not to say anything about our worship of Mithras. Finding three grown men together in a darkened room might have given him some ideas!"

Versillius chose to ignore the final comment. He could see that the Paribius and Domitius were visibly shocked to hear the news of the latest killing.

"Another murder is the last thing that our settlement needs," the money lender responded, as he placed his goose quill pen on the desk, "But on the bright side, the less civic officials there are, the fewer taxes we will have to pay..."

The centurion glared at the man, angrily.

"I'm sorry," Paribius continued, as he saw the expression on the soldier's face, "I didn't really mean that at all. Versillius, please forgive me...you know what an indiscreet tongue that I have. If only my mind worked half as swiftly as my mouth."

"Partimius was a good man and your comments were uncalled for. Now, I need to see your petition," the centurion replied. Paribius nodded and placed the quill pen into an inkwell, before wiping his hands on his trousers. He then held up eight large sheets of vellum and handed them over to the centurion. The value of the parchment must have been almost equal to that of their increased tax bill. Most citizens wrote on thin sheets of wooden tablets, which cost next to nothing. Versillius looked at the thickness of the petition and considered the fact that the ink on the last sheet of vellum was still damp. In his opinion, it was a weighty submission. It was of sufficient length to have taken the three men two late nights to compose. Handing the document back to Paribius he said,

"Hands, gentlemen, please. I want to see your hands."

One by one, they obeyed his instruction and presented their hands to him. Looking closely at their finger nails, the centurion could detect no signs of blood, between the nail and flesh. He was sure that the killing and depositing of Partimius on the funeral pyre would have left bloodstains on his assailants' hands. Especially with the messy wound to the stomach, not all the blood could have been easily washed away. The only substance that Versillius could see on the three men's hands, were ink marks. This proved that they had taken it in turns to write their petition. He then looked their togas up and down, carefully noting that he could detect no signs of blood or dirt. The garments were, however, creased and had obviously been worn all day. The centurion nodded and told them, "And now for your boots. I want to see the bottom of your footwear."

Unable to help himself, Paribius raised his eyebrows, at the mention of the word 'bottom'. Fortunately, he managed to stifle a grin, as he could see that the legionnaire was in no mood for humour. Vespasianus and Domitius looked puzzled at this request. But the three men stood, side by side, at the desk. In turn, one foot at a time, they raised their feet behind them. Versillius looked at each boot intently. The soles and the tops of their footwear were clean. This was unlike the centurion's caligulae, which were coated with mud from the cemetery. The crematorium's proximity to the spring made it susceptible to being very muddy. Turning to the three traders, he said, "Whoever killed Antonius also murdered the junior scribe. I'm now satisfied that the three of you have been here all night. Which eliminates you from my enquiries..."

"Who did it then?" Domitius asked.

"I still have six suspects left on my list and do not want to alert any of them. So I'll say goodnight and see you at the latrines in the morning."

"Whoever is responsible," Vespasianus stated, "You need to catch them quickly, before any more citizens are murdered. If I were you, then I would start with your soldier, Trajanius."

"Why do you think that?" the centurion asked.

"Well, you were the one who was asking questions about Mithras, earlier today. When I refused to join the cult, or contribute to it financially, Trajanius dropped his jovial recruitment act. Suddenly, rather being promised a meeting with the pater, I was being threatened with his displeasure..."

"Vespasianus, it might have helped if you had told me this before," Versillius interrupted, "Why didn't you tell me about it, when I first interviewed you?"

"I do not know who this pater figure is, so I was reluctant to come forward. But now that there has been another murder, well that makes everything different, doesn't it?" the merchant answered. For once, a tone of uncertainty was evident in his voice.

He was backed up by wholehearted nods of agreement, from his two colleagues. They had obviously received the same offers and threats from Trajanius. Versillius made a mental note to conduct his next interview with the legionnaire as a matter of some urgency. This time his surly, barrack room magistrate attitude would not protect him. And unless the centurion received far better answers this time round, then Trajanius could expect a worse punishment than being told to complete his duty.

"He also tried to get me to join," Paribius volunteered, "But with my delicate posterior, there was no way that I could undergo a beating ritual. And the pitiful state of my finances prevented me from helping financially. I got threatened as well. Perhaps, I too should have told you this sooner?"

The look on the centurion's face told the money lender that he should have done. But before departing, Versillius had some important personal business to conclude. So he said to Paribius. "Partimius owed you money for his thatched house. I intend to make those payments on Getilla's behalf. Just tell me how much and when in the month it falls due." Versillius then left the traders to finish their work on the petition. As he departed, he heard just a few mutterings about the wasting of taxpayer's money and a comment about himself and Getilla. But feeling pleased that he had managed to rule out three suspects, he finally decided to spend the rest of the night in his villa. The lateness of the hour and the fatigue in his body had influenced his decision. More importantly, the centurion knew that neither the legate nor the prefect would think to look for him there. He would confront them in the morning, when he would be fresher and rested. As for Trajanius, it would also be better to confront him, after a good night's sleep. Whether the soldier was involved in the killings was now irrelevant. Threatening citizens, particularly important and influential citizens, was more than enough for him to take his centurion's vine stick out of the cupboard. Versillius then dusted it down and mimed a few hard, well aimed swishes at an imaginary Trajanius with it.

Chapter Seventeen

It was early when the centurion rose and returned to the barracks, approaching the fort by the via south. In the forum, there was still the market traders' refuse for citizens to contend with. But that had dropped way down on his list of problems. Even though he had eliminated the three traders from the murder enquiry, thanks to the death of Partimius, he still had six more suspects to consider. Of these one was Artemis, who he had almost eliminated from the investigation the previous afternoon. The demise of the junior scribe also seemed to eliminate the priestess from the list. Other than Trajanius, that left three suspects. But they were three very powerful men. And he had no doubt that they would want to see him very soon. His assumption was not misplaced. As he entered the barracks, through the southern gate, Marcus approached him and said, "Thank the deities, that you are back! The prefect is already here, along with the governor and legate. All three are demanding to see you, as soon as possible. They were furious that you were not in the barracks overnight. The general even mentioned that your absence could be considered as a dereliction of duty."

After his efforts of the previous day, Versillius was in no mood to be browbeaten by the senior officials or officers. Especially as he saw them as suspects in a double murder case. He replied to Marcus, "Thanks for the warning, it is appreciated. Now, please take me to them. Where exactly are the three buzzards hovering?"

"In your office, sir. They've been there for nearly an hour now..."

"That's fine, don't worry, I can handle their gripes. But first listen, when they've had their say, we really need to speak to Trajanius. Last night, I found out that he has actually been threatening the traders who refused to join his little sect!"

Marcus seemed less than surprised by this and answered, "And yesterday, Partimius told us that he had threatened Antonius. I'll go and get him for you right away. When you are finished with the inquisitors, he will be waiting outside your private quarters. If I am permitted, then I would like to assist in his second interview, sir!" the younger soldier said. The two men then entered the barracks together, but leaving Marcus behind, the centurion walked into his office. It was a small room, close to the main entrance. As the young soldier had warned him the reception committee was anxiously awaiting his arrival. The first person to speak was the general, Appius Severus, who was sat behind Versillius' own desk. He raised himself up and said, "It's very kind of you to give us some of your valuable time, Versillius. I must repay the complement soon. In fact, I think that I will do it right now. From the moment of my arrival in Virulanium, I had thought that the day of your retirement had already arrived. In my confusion, I spent the evening in the belief that the fort was without a centurion! But both the governor and the prefect assured me that was not the case, despite the evidence of my own eyes."

Appius Severus was a man of medium height, who had a classical and very large Roman nose. Versillius did not reply to his taunts, contenting himself with a look of distaste. The commanding officer was unusual in this extremity of the empire, having been born in Rome, to a patrician family. The story prevalent in the twentieth legion was that as a young officer and political appointee, his sharp tongue had been rather too sharp. So sharp in fact, that he had offended the late emperor, Constantine the first. Rather than having him executed, the ruler had permanently exiled him to Britannia as a form of punishment. Away from the imperial city and any thought of political advancement, he had been given command of the twentieth legion. But there was now much talk that he was hopeful of a return to the imperial city. Earlier in the year, the usurper Magnentius had murdered and seized the western throne from the legitimate emperor. This was Constans the first, the son of Constantine. With the Constantine dynasty apparently at an end, the legate's return seemed assured. Well at least that was what the latest army gossip had to say, Versillius reminded himself, as he remained silent.

"Have you lost your tongue, officer?" The general continued, "Surely, when your commanding officer speaks, you should reply! Or is there no such thing as military discipline in Virulanium any longer?"

Still saying nothing, Versillius looked the man up and down. The centurion was convinced that the commanding officer's curly brown hair was too brown to be natural for a man of over 50 years of age. Refusing to be bullied, Versillius held his tongue. Eventually, when he was ready, the centurion said, "I have been working very hard at solving a double murder. It was two hours before the sun rose that I managed to retire to my villa and get some sleep. Before that, I had to comfort the latest victim's widow and for good measure, I also managed to clear three suspects..."

"Why wasn't I told immediately about the death of Partimius?" the prefect cut in, his bottom lip trembling.

"Because by the time I had finished my duties, on the eastern side of the vicus, the hour was very late. And besides, I knew that you had been entertaining our high status guests all night. In all likelihood, you would all have been asleep at that time." was his reply.

"That didn't stop you from disturbing me on the night when Antonius was killed. I'll talk to you later Versillius!" the prefect, Gaius Flavius countered.

The legate smiled at the centurion and said, "I'll leave it for you to sort out your differences with the prefect later. But Versillius, do you want to know what I think? I can see straight away that your face tells me that you do not. But I will speak and you will listen, soldier. This so-called murder case that you are investigating is a complete waste of time. All that you and your subordinate are doing is annoying the honest traders of Virulanium. From the moment that I heard about the first killing, I realised that it was the Picts who were responsible. The location of the second murder, just south of the Wall, merely confirms my suspicions."

Both the governor and the prefect glanced at each other and the former, a tall, mild mannered man, started to say, "But there is evidence to the contrary, Appius Severus. There are missing papers and purses, not to mention keys to the civic buildings..."

"Quintus Lucius, at times you are as much of a fool as this centurion is," the legate interjected, "Are you really prepared to listen to his ill conceived ramblings, rather than accept my considered judgement? Tell me, just who is in charge here?"

"I have not had a chance to hear the centurion, but his junior officer fully briefed me on the evidence that they had found," the governor replied, obviously annoyed at the way that he had been addressed.

"The governor is right, Appius Severus," the prefect said, "There are some things about these killings that do not ring true. It seems as if the fatal wounds were inflicted by a Roman sword."

The commanding officer rose to his feet, shaking his head. He stared at the prefect before admonishing him, by saying, "You too, Gaius Flavius. I honestly thought better of your judgement. Perhaps the rain in this part of the world has made your brains go soft as well. Let us all remember that the barbarians have been raiding us for hundreds of years. Surely, it is it not beyond the realms of possibility that they may have stolen the odd gladius? After all they steal our cattle, sheep, provisions and anything else that they can lay their hands on!"

As the three officials argued amongst themselves, Versillius pondered on their relationship. In theory the governor, Quintus Lucius, was in charge of all matters along the Wall. But his personality was such that he was unable to stand up to the patrician and opinionated legate. The prefect certainly had the temper and drive, but as a civic official, he did not have the authority to over rule the legion's commander. Deciding to throw caution to the wind, the centurion said, "So I take it that you gentlemen are not concerned about your missing private papers? They were sent to the chief scribe only two days ago and now there is no trace of them..."

Appius Severus, who was still on his feet, answered, "The idiot probably misplaced them. Anyway we have only the word of a dead man that they were in his office at all, which hardly strikes me as conclusive evidence. They could well be in some other room in the civic building, awaiting delivery or maybe even in his villa."

"So what do you suggest that we do?" the governor asked, tentatively, not wanting another verbal battering.

"I'll tell you what I suggest" the general replied and hesitated for a second before continuing, " No, what I command! Versillius will take a punitive patrol across the border, to the nearest Pict settlement. You will exact revenge and show these barbarians that we are not to be taken lightly. Burn their village and slaughter everybody. Then these incursions and killings will stop. I would think that twenty legionnaires should be sufficient to carry out the task."

"So you are not of the opinion that the killer could be in our midst?" the prefect said.

"Of course not and may I remind you, Gaius Flavius, that military matters are my responsibility and mine alone. Perhaps, you'd be better off recruiting some new scribes, to keep your administration from grinding to a halt. It would suit your prospects better than offering me useless advice, on issues that do not concern you! Remember, that my only reason for visiting this dismal place, is that I have an important civic inspection and audit to carry out," was the general's terse and exasperated reply.

The centurion watched with interest, as the prefect's face turned several shades of purple and his body shuddered with suppressed anger. But somehow keeping himself under control, his skin eventually lightened to its normal ruddy complexion and Gaius Flavius was eventually able to reply calmly, "There are still some officials left, Appius Severus. Rest assured, that they will be at your disposal, as will I, when our services are required."

"I'm glad to hear it," the general replied nonchalantly, before turning to the centurion and resuming, "You will go and muster your force. Don't forget, I said no more than twenty men. That should be more than enough to teach these savages a lesson, which they will not relish. Now that we all understand each other clearly, you are can both leave and set about your duties, Gaius Flavius and Versillius."

Having issues his orders, the legate paused for a moment before addressing the governor, "Now then, Quintus Lucius, my dear, old fellow, I think we'll have a swift chat about official business. But afterwards, don't you think it will be time for us to bathe, now that I have sorted these two incompetents out?"

Rather than replying, Quintus Lucius merely twitched nervously and nodded his assent. The two incompetents walked out of the centurion's office glaring at each other. Both were very anxious to get outside the office and resume their earlier conversation well away from the legate's earshot.

Chapter Eighteen

Marcus was waiting for them just outside the centurion's office. After summoning Trajanius, he had ordered the soldier to stand outside Versillius' private quarters. The legionnaire had then returned to the corridor. As the two men emerged, it was obvious that the meeting had not gone well. He could see straight away that the prefect was in one of his many less than good moods. Marcus could also sense that Versillius was not too pleased either. The young man could understand why, because he had overheard most of what had been said by the legate. With a feeling of trepidation, he hesitated as first the centurion and then the prefect approached him.

"I want the pair of you to come with me, now!" Gaius Flavius hissed at them, the moment that the door was closed. Still fuming from the legate's dressing down, he lead the two legionnaires to a quieter part of the barracks before saying to Versillius, "Centurion, don't you ever put me in such a position again. If anything serious happens in this settlement, then I need to know about it, whatever the time of night or day! And I don't care who I am entertaining or how hard you may have worked or even how tired you were."

Versillius was also furious at the high handed treatment handed out by the general. But he was no longer prepared to let the prefect take his anger out on him. So he replied, "Why do you need to know about anything that happens in Virulanium, Gaius Flavius? Can you tell me the exact point of keeping you informed about events?"

"Because I do not intend to be humiliated again in front of the legate and governor, in such a manner.

You should know that by now, and I must say that your effrontery..."

"I'm sorry for you embarrassment, prefect, but what I'll tell you exactly what I know," the centurion stated firmly, cutting him short, "Marcus and I spent more than a day gathering evidence, which has now been totally disregarded. But it turns out that we were wasting our time. I didn't notice you telling the legate anything much about that. All that I saw and heard, and in my own office too, was you and the governor offering to kiss his..."

"That's enough, Versillius, I don't want to hear another word on this subject," Gaius Flavius yelled, "I tried to point out to him about the victims' gladius wounds and..."

"I didn't see you trying very hard. You muttered a few words and so did the governor. Then the two of you let him take a civil investigation into the realm of the military. Very well, I'll lead detail of twenty men and we'll go and slaughter a few Picts. But you know as well as I do, that it will not solve these murders. It certainly won't prevent any further killings in Virulanium from happening."

"I have already told you, centurion, that you have spoken enough. It appears to me, that your retirement is long overdue," the prefect responded. Although the look on his now gaunt, rather than usually ruddy, face showed that he was relying on the authority of his office, rather than the force of his argument.

"You do not have to wait long for that, prefect, just a couple of months. Now if you will excuse me, I have a legionnaire to discipline and a punitive detail to organise," was the centurion's terse reply.

The prefect shook his head and replied in a calmer, but still slightly exasperated voice, "I can't let you go on the punitive detail, with us at loggerheads. Please, let us just agree to disagree on this issue and not let it come between us. I'm afraid to tell you that my wife has decided that tonight we must host a full feast for the occasion of the legate's visit. She's had the servants and slaves working on it full time since he arrived in Virulanium, and she asked me to invite you. For some reason, which I certainly do not understand, she has always had a soft spot for you, Versillius. I suppose you'll be back from across the border by nightfall?"

The centurions tone was also more measured, as he replied to Gaius Flavius, realising that their argument was over, "If I'm still in one piece, after the incursion, then I will be there. Please, thank your wife for her kindness. Now, can we go and get the punitive party organised? No offence, prefect, but these things are best done sooner rather than later."

"Yes, you'd better go and get this over with. But believe me, when I say that I am no greater an admirer of Appius Lucius than you are. Just be careful with yourself, Versillius, and come back to Virulanium in good shape. You too Marcus..."

The prefect then handed Versillius the invitation from his wife. It was written in ink, on a small wooden tablet of pressed elder. Due to the lack of papyrus and the cost of parchment, this was the medium used by literate citizens to send each other personal communications. While the centurion glanced at the invitation, Gaius Flavius left the barracks. As he entered the forum, the official saw that he was not far behind the general and the governor. They had finished their business and were heading towards the bathhouses. Keeping his distance from the pair of them, the white haired official veered off in the direction of the civic buildings. Once inside, he knew that he would be able to calm down completely in the sanctity of his office. The prefect smiled at the irony of his behaviour. In the fort, he had the reputation of being a man who would cross the forum to have an argument with himself. Yet here he was, hiding from Appius Severus. He sincerely hoped that the story about the legate returning to Rome, had more than a grain of truth in. If it did, then until a replacement commander arrived, his life would be so much easier with only the governor to deal with. And it was always possible that Rome would not send them such another arse with ears, he told himself.

Meanwhile, in the barracks, Marcus had been sent to round up seventeen soldiers to carry out the legate's instructions. Versillius had told his subordinate that he was more than capable of dealing with Trajanius on his own. He apologised to the younger man, for denying him the pleasure of attending the interview and returned to his own quarters. Trajanius was waiting outside the door, half standing and half slouching against the plain brick wall. But on seeing the centurion, he stood to attention, his arms by his side and said almost respectfully, "Good morning, sir! How is our commanding officer, sir? I had heard that he was rather anxious to see you."

Versillius was slightly puzzled at his approach. He had not been expecting to find a contrite and subservient Trajanius. But surely the man ought to be more concerned for his own prospects, rather than the well being of the legate? The centurion replied, "We are detailed to take a punitive party across the border. You will be part of it, when I have finished with you. Marcus is organising the other members."

"So it was the Picts that killed the scribes then? I thought that all along..."

"If you thought that all along," Versillius interjected, "Why didn't you think to inform me before? As I recall, we had a conversation on the night of Antonius' murder. But you didn't say a single word about our northern neighbours."

"That's because you were accusing me of being involved," Trajanius responded, his manner now less than certain and still markedly less surly than it usually was. The centurion smiled at him and said, "I still am accusing you. Tell me, what were you doing last night, at the time that Partimius was killed? And I do not want any lies, as I know that your night duty finished on the previous day!"

The legionnaire was slightly disconcerted, by this direct question. He had to think for a few moments, before saying, "If you must know, I was conducting an initiation ceremony. Although, it's none of your business what I do in my own time!"

"You are wrong there, soldier. Until you leave the army, everything that you do is my business. Especially, when you start to threaten prominent members of this community, because they will not subscribe to your misplaced belief in Mithras!"

"I've...I've..er...done nothing of the sort," Trajanius countered, his usual confidence and cockiness, now completely gone.

"Well I have heard otherwise and from more than one person. When we return from our raid, I shall get to the bottom of this. And that includes finding out who this so important pater figure is. Do I make myself clear?" Trajanius could see that Versillius was deadly serious. He grimaced, pulled at the skin around his throat and answered, "I'll go and get ready for our expedition, sir. But if I was you, then I wouldn't be too inquisitive about the pater. You may be my centurion, but he is far more powerful than you are. I can't say who he is, but I will say that our religion has the support of the proconsul in *Eboracum*."

Versillius watched as Trajanius departed, his cockiness and arrogance suddenly back in full flow. If the legionnaire was speaking the truth, something that he always doubted, then he had just implicated the most senior imperial official in Northern Britannia.

Chapter Nineteen

The soldier's words merely confirmed Versillius' suspicions that it was a person of high rank who was behind the two murders. But as he had to go and slaughter some Picts, he decided to let matters rest, for the time being. It was time for him to prepare for battle. As far as he was concerned, the enquiry would be pursued if and when he returned to the fort. Alone in his chambers, the centurion started to put out his weapons and armour. On the march, a Roman soldier carried or wore equipment that weighed about sixty pounds. So for convenience, when he was not on active duty the centurion, like the rest of his men, was happy to wear trousers, a belted tunica and a toga. If the weather was particularly cold or wet, he would throw a paenula cloak around his shoulders. But going into battle or any potentially hostile situation was a different matter entirely.

Although, he had taken off his civilian belt and toga, Versillius did not remove his thick, woollen trousers. They were staying on, along with his red tunica. At one time a legionnaire would not have considered wearing trousers, but that was in the hot climate of the Mediterranean. Even this far north, their use had originally been seen as somewhat effeminate, until years of exposure to cold and wet weather had made people see sense. Now, soldiers and civilians alike wore them without encountering as much as a raised eyebrow. However, he did remove his socks and *caligae*, the hob-nailed legionnaires' boots, which had an open toe and heel. Reaching into a drawer, on the far side of the room, he removed a large bulb of garlic and broke off eight cloves. After he had crushed them with his fingers, they were placed between his toes before he pulled his socks back on. It was an old soldiers' trick, which alleviated the pain suffered by the feet, in the course of a long march.

Having replaced his caligae, the centurion picked then up his military *cingulum* belt. This was made of leather, with drawstrings at the rear and embossed with copper plates. At its front, hung five thin leather strips, which were covered with metal. The sporran shaped device acted as a protector, for that most delicate of areas, the soldier's groin and testicles. The belt also supported the sheath, which held his *pugio*, or multi purpose dagger, which could be used for combat or eating. Having secured the cingulum around his midriff, he then pulled on his *subarmalis*, or protective leather vest. It was worn to protect a soldier's body and shoulders from the chaffing of his armour. The garment also protected the armour, from rusting which could be easily caused by a legionnaire's sweat or blood.

Next he secured the *greaves* or metal leg protectors around his lower legs. These were traditionally worn by centurions, rather than their legionnaires. Although, he drew the line at wearing the officer's protective arm guards. This was because he preferred to have freedom of movement when he was wielding his gladius. It was now time for him to put on the *segmentata,* metal body armour, which was secured by leather ties and straps. Most of his men wore the *maile* armour shirts, which were comprised of linked metal rings. They were cheaper and easier to obtain than segmented armour and effective against slashing blows. But maile offered no protestation against piercing or stabbing blows. Which was exactly why Versillius had chosen to buy and wear the segmented plate armour. Raising the plates above his head, he gently lowered the metal strips onto his shoulders. The centurion then adjusted the leather straps, as best he could. Marcus could finish the final adjustments, on the parade ground, before he addressed the detail.

Then, he put on his *baldric* belt, a narrow leather strap, which was worn over the shoulder and housed the sheathed gladius. This was followed by his cloak, which was tied loosely around his shoulders and trailed behind him. Finally, Versillius took up his plumed helmet. Like his armour, this was distinct to those worn by his men, due to the centurion's red horsehair plume. It was mounted horizontally, across the centre of the helmet, rather than vertically from front to rear. In some ways, it fulfilled the function of the greaves and arm guards, easily identifying a centurion to the men under his command. Before leaving his rooms, Versillius picked up his *scutum* or shield. This was a large, wooden oval shape and edged with rawhide. Unlike the classical rectangular shields, which were made of glued wooden strips, these were less cumbersome and cheaper to make.

Cheaper to make. Those words ran through the centurion's mind, as he walked out of the barracks towards the parade ground. A legionnaire had to buy his own weapons and equipment, the cost of which was deducted from his pay. But now there was no decent armour or equipment to be purchased. His own segmentata was over a hundred years old and had at least three previous owners. Although, it had cost him a small fortune, at least it was reliable and offered good upper body protection. But some of his men could not even afford to buy the maile shirts. Their upper body protection was supplied by strips of metal, cannibalised from old segmentata and cobbled together by the local blacksmith. The laws of economics also applied to the swords that were now forged. Versillius insisted upon his men using the short gladius and the older the better. In his younger days, he had seen many of the long spathae shatter after one blow against an enemy's shield. The men also had similar problems with their oval shields. The army's traditional rectangles had been laminated and absorbed blows with more resilience than the plank built oval shapes.

But he had to put all his thoughts of exasperation to one side, when he arrived at the parade ground. Marcus had mustered the force, who were prepared and armed, as best as they could be. The soldiers, Trajanius included, stood to attention as he approached them. Telling the men to stand at ease, he called Marcus over to him. As the younger man adjusted the straps on his armour, he asked the centurion, in a very low voice, "How did your interview with Trajanius go, sir?"

"He payed out the rope and wrapped it around his neck. I was informed that the pater is a far more important man than I am. He may even be the proconsul. But that's for later. I have to address the detail now."

Standing in front of the legionnaires, Versillius explained the legate's orders and the purpose of their mission. For once, there was no heckling or muttering from any of them. They all stood in complete silence, listening intently to their commanding officer's words. Trajanius was no exception. The centurion was slightly nonplussed by this, but continued with his address. When he had finished, he gave the order to gather up weapons and prepare for the march. Most of the legionnaires received his orders with a customary stoicism and a willingness to get an unpleasant job done. The centurion watched, as they checked their equipment for the final time. He assumed that their compliant attitude could only be put down to boredom. At least this mission was a change from mounting guard duties or repairing the Wall.

All the men knew that the nearest Pictish village was less than five miles to the north of the Wall. At marching pace that should take them only an hour and a forty minutes. A legionnaire was expected to cover a mile in twenty minutes on uneven terrain. On good Roman roads, troops were expected to cover four miles in an hour, at full pace. Then there was the matter of the battle to fight and conclude. Versillius estimated that there would be at most, a further hour to teach the barbarians the legate's lesson. He then added on another hour and a forty minutes to return. If all went well they should be back in the fort by mid afternoon. He had Marcus form the men into three ranks of six, and took the lead point. With the younger man at his side, he marched the troops out of the fort, by the north gate. As they entered the territory of the Picts, Marcus said to him, "While you were preparing for our mission, Getilla arrived with her father and brothers. I allowed them to remove Partimius' body, so that they could take it to the funeral pyre. Hopefully, we'll both avoid the need for such a structure to be built for ourselves today."

"I have no great fear of that," the centurion replied, "My main worry is that there are far greater dangers for us to confront on our own side of the wall, when we return..."

Chapter Twenty

On the northern side of the border, beyond the Wall, there were no roads. Just trails, which had been trodden into the grass of the fields, by other such details of legionnaires who had headed north. For over two hundred years, the Picts and their predecessors had fought the Romans in this border area. Although Versillius had spoken the truth, when he told Marcus that the emperor Hadrian had wanted the Wall to define the empire's northern boundary, it also served another practical purpose. Even when the Scots managed to cross it, then they were unable to rustle Romano-British livestock. Not even the strongest of the savages was able to lift a cow or sheep over the structure, provided it was kept in a good state of repair. Which, was why in recent times they, had started to steal provisions and property from Virulanium and other vicii. But to his knowledge and despite the legate's strong words, the murdering of scribes was a brand new sideline for the northern barbarians.

His detachment made rapid progress through the fields and over the hills, even though the rain had returned. Undulating green countryside and grey skies would always be the centurion's abiding memory of the territory to the north of the wall. The men maintained full marching pace, almost as if they were walking on solid Roman roads. Versillius glanced behind him and was pleased to see that they were keeping their ranks and in good order. It was a sign that not all the hours of drilling on the parade ground had been wasted. Their training would be an important factor when they reached the Picts' settlement and went into battle. He also took the opportunity to look around at the rugged beauty of the countryside that they were marching through and tried to appreciate it. And due to the rain, failed.

The centurion also found the complete silence very unnerving. There was no sign of man, beast or bird so everything was totally quiet. That would be at least until they arrived at their destination. Of course, the irony of Appius Severus ordering them into battle with the Scots was not lost on the centurion. From what he knew, the closest that the legate had ever come to a sword blow was when he had watched the gladiators fight, in Rome or Londinium. But these thoughts were suddenly interrupted, by Marcus, who asked him, "So which three suspects did you clear last night, sir? I've been waiting to ask, since we left the fort, but saw that you were lost in contemplation."

The centurion smiled at him and explained about his visit to Vespasianus' villa and the size of their petition. The young soldier had to agree that the lack of blood under their fingernails, coupled with the ink stains on their hands was fairly conclusive. Especially, when considered alongside the facts that the three traders were wearing creased, but clean clothes and their boots that had no mud on them. In a quiet voice he went onto say, "So that just leaves us with Trajanius, the priestess, doctor and the unholy triumvirate, one of whom who sent us out on this mission. What do you think, sir?"

Versillius replied, "The doctor had no axe or gladius to grind against Partimius, so we also can rule him out. The junior scribe wouldn't have said boo to himself, let alone criticise our physician. That was Antonius' pastime. But I can't entirely rule out the priestess at the moment, even though I was minded to earlier. Remember that it would have been Partimius, who would have to pursue the writ of confiscation that

that his former superior had launched against the temple."

"You have a point there," Marcus responded, " But surely it would mean that she would have to kill or dispose of every chief scribe that was ever appointed. Where would that all end, with ten or twenty murders? Or, perhaps, nobody from Virulanium or the surrounding area, would ever apply for the post of scribe, because of the dangers involved?"

The centurion hadn't previously realised that his junior had a sense of humour and a fine wit. He laughed at the concept of scribing being potentially more fatal than the work that they were about to carry out and said, "If you are right, then we can strike not only the doctor, but the priestess from our list. That leaves us with Trajanius and what you called the unholy triumvirate and the Christians call the holy trinity. And if Trajanius was telling me the truth then we cannot rule out the proconsul's involvement. Legionnaire, prefect, governor, legate or proconsul. Which one is your money on? Because I am sure that money is the key to this case. Remember, the scrap of parchment that we found in Partimius' hand had just one word on it; *solidus*."

"I noticed that you didn't mention that to the legate earlier. Not that I was listening, but your voices were so loud that I couldn't help but overhear..." as Marcus finished talking, a sheepish grin flickered across his features.

"Stop playing the fool," Versillius said, "In your position, I would have been pressed up against the office door as closely as possible. With your intelligence and aptitude, I would be very disappointed to find out that you did not do the same. Now, tell me, did you inform any of them about the piece of vellum?"

"No, not at all. I thought it would be better coming from you, as the senior officer, in charge of the case. Besides, we had already identified them as potential suspects. When they arrived at the barracks I only briefed them about the actual murder of Partimius. I kept quiet about the evidence. Whatever the legate says, resolving this investigation means as much to me, as it does to you, centurion."

They had been marching for some time now. Versillius realised that the Picts' village could not be far off. So he broke off his conversation with Marcus and halting the patrol and said, "Listen men, if the barbarians haven't been spotted us already, then they soon will. When we come under attack, I will take the right flank of the first wave and Marcus will take the left. As long as we keep our shields interlocked we should be fine. I want to see your *pila* take out more than a few Picts, before we have to draw our swords. Is that understood?"

Now that they were some distance from the fort, the legionnaires' initial confidence had been replaced with a nervous edginess. But the soldiers still nodded their agreement at his words, before resuming the march. Versillius had not been wrong in his assessment of their position. After they had crossed the next range of hills, the Pict's village came into sight. It was a collection of small to medium sized, round houses, which were encircled by a raised earth bank. Smoke was rising though the thatched roofs, as the settlement's inhabitants cooked the day's food. To Versillius it looked like a picture of basic, rustic simplicity and calm. But massed directly before him, there was now a force of some fifty angry and agitated barbarians to consider. They were armed with small round shields, spears and long slashing swords. So much for rustic simplicity, peace and calm, the centurion thought to himself. Surveying the enemy, it only took Versillius one swift glance, to see that there was not a single enemy wielding a gladius. He breathed deeply, to prepare himself for combat, as the Picts yelled and mounted their charge towards the legionnaires.

Chapter Twenty One

Despite the disparity in their forces, Versillius was not over perturbed, because the Picts were advancing towards them without any order or discipline. In all his years of guarding the Wall, the centurion had never known the northerners to show even a basic grasp of military tactics. Their only battle plan was to run at the enemy, yelling very loudly and swinging their long swords around their heads. It was as if they wanted to engage the opposition in hand-to-hand combat, in some sort of macho ego trip. But a Roman legion did not function in that way. The well-trained and disciplined legionnaires would carry out their pre-ordained battle plan. So the centurion shouted quite calmly, to the soldiers under his command, "Stop marching and keep your cool, men. There's nothing for you to be afraid of here. Now, first rank, I want you to lock your shields."

Having issued his orders, he moved a few steps back, to join the right flank. Simultaneously, Marcus moved to the left, and they stood behind their shields. Each man pressed his shield against that of the man stood next to him. The first rank now formed a solid wall of eight tall, oval shields. "They are coming onto us, so we must hold the line," the centurion said, again in a measured way, "Ranks two and three, lock your shields. And I want every man in the second and third rank to ready his pila. Throw the heavy *pilum* first. "

The legionnaires carried two types of javelins or pila. Both were designed so that their metal tips would bend, after they had been thrown. This meant that the weapon could not be picked up by the enemy and hurled back at the legionnaires. But the heavy pilum was a deadly weapon, because of the large lead weight, which was positioned behind its iron tip. With sufficient momentum, it was powerful enough to pierce an adversary's shield or the armour that he was wearing. Although, as the Picts were virtually naked, from the waist up, Versillius fully expected the heavy javelin to be far more deadly, than it normally was. Following his instructions, the men to the rear formed into their battle formation. The twenty Roman soldiers then awaited the onrushing Picts, knowing that their tall oval shields and three ranks presented a formidable barricade. They also saw that the northern men were not armoured and realised that their smaller, round shields would not give the same protection as the legionnaire's large oval scutum.

From his position on the right flank Versillius could see the attackers' uncovered blue torsos, as they advanced. As the Picts moved forward, they shouted and mouthed obscenities that he could not understand. The savages spoke a strange language that no Roman and few Britons could comprehend. He ignored the ferocity of their barbaric utterings and waited, content that they were attacking his detachment and playing into his hands. When they were within eighty yards of the legionnaires, the centurion realised that the Picts were about to unleash a volley of their spears. "Place your javelins on the ground, men, it's time to cover up," he said loudly, "I think that they are about to throw their spears at us."

At his instruction, the front rank knelt down. They placed their shields vertically on the ground for protection and took shelter behind them. The second and third ranks also knelt down on the ground. But they raised their shields above their own heads, so that they also covered the men in front of them. The soldiers had formed the classical Roman army's defensive armadillo shape. When the anticipated volley of spears arrived, it bounced harmlessly off their protected ranks. The centurion knew that it was now time to make their javelins count, as the Picts were quickly closing in on them very quickly. They were now just fifty yards away, the optimum distance for the pilum, so he yelled, "At the double, I want every man stood up. Unleash your heavy javelins."

To a man, the Roman soldiers rose and hurled a hail of their heavy pointed weapons. As it landed, the centurion saw at least eight barbarians fall. Unlike the Romans, their adversaries had no concept of an interlocking wall of shields. They also had another big disadvantage. Whereas they carried only one long wooden spear, a legionnaire had two javelins in his possession, which were smaller in length and easier to transport across rough terrain. The second volley that the soldiers threw was just as murderous in its intensity. More of the enemy fell to the ground with mortal or serious wounds inflicted by the slender pila. The centurion was pleased because the odds were rapidly coming down in his favour. Their opponents suddenly halted in their stride, fearing another onslaught, as they realised that they were taking heavy casualties. "Draw the gladius, men," he said, noting the enemy's uncertainty and hesitation, "Relock your shields and let us move forward to finish the job."

With their oval shields to the fore, the three ranks unsheathed their swords. They were held at waist height, in the soldiers' right hands. Each man's shield was to his left, partially protecting his neighbour, as the short, stabbing gladius extended forwards. The legionnaires banged the sword on the side of their shields, making the menacing sound of a military drumbeat. Then advancing one step at a time, left foot first, they faced the regrouping Picts. They had now resumed their charge and had drawn the long swords, which were being waved wildly, above their heads. When the two forces clashed head on the Roman soldier's training held them in good stead, as they let their shields absorb the initial onslaught. Then the legionnaires got to work, still walking slowly, one pace at a time, but the front rank thrusting the gladius in time with their movements. Against a body of men, pressed up against them, the short sword did its murderous work. The remaining savages were too compacted to use their longer weapons to any good effect.

At the centurion's command, the second and third ranks performed a flanking movement to the left and right hand sides. Advancing swiftly, they attacked the enemy's flanks, with each man pushing his shield into the body of an opponent. This had the effect of knocking the enemy off balance, allowing the Roman soldier to thrust his gladius into the disoriented man's stomach or side. The momentum of their charge, against the single rank, funnelled the surviving Picts into a packet that was surrounded on three sides. Caught by surprise, the barbarians panicked and ran, but not before many of their number had been cut down. Seeing that the survivors were in full retreat, Versillius raised his sword in the air. The centurion swirled it in a circular motion, signifying that the action was over. As he glanced at the patrol, making a quick head count, he was pleased to see that they had taken no casualties. One or two men had the odd scratch or cut, but that was the extent of the injuries suffered. The armadillo shaped wall of shields had yet again done its protective job against an enemy's spears. Roman discipline and training had then prevailed against the spatha. However, it was an entirely different matter for the Scots, as Versillius was able to count at least twenty bodies, which were lying bleeding on the green turf.

As he made the gesture, the men let up the cheer of victory. They pointed their swords in the direction of the fleeing enemy and shouted their own profanities at them, which the Picts would not understand. This struck Versillius as one of the main problems to the two peoples not being able to live in peace. Neither side could understand a single word that the other was saying, obscene or otherwise. With the battle was now concluded, he removed his helmet and watched as his soldiers despatched the badly wounded and groaning Picts, with their swords. That was standard army practice, so he had no qualms about it. Had they lost, then the savages would have done the same to his wounded men. While the sweat was drying on his brow, Trajanius, approached Versillius and said, "Are we going on to burn their village, sir? We've obviously got them on the run, there could be woman and plunder to be had!"

The centurion did not even need to think for a single second, before responding, "My instructions, from the legate, were to teach them a lesson. I think that more than twenty dead Picts is a good reminder of our ways. Their village will suffer enough, now that almost half their men folk are dead. But if you really want to do something useful, break their swords and spears into two. Then, they can never be used against us again."

"But the legate wanted us to burn their village..."

"Tell me, how you do you know that?" Versillius interrupted, "As you were not present at the meeting. While I was receiving the legate's instructions, you were waiting outside my private quarters, which are on the opposite side of the barracks!"

"I...I thought that was what you told us at the briefing, on the parade ground. If we're not going to burn them out, then I'll go and break some weapons."

The self-proclaimed runner of the sun departed quickly, leaving Versillius to ponder on just what the legionnaire knew. And more importantly, whom he was getting his information from. Putting this to one side, he glanced up at the Picts' village. He could see men, women and children leaving their round houses and heading north. They obviously expected the worst and were fleeing from their homes. The centurion asked himself if these people were really the descendants of the Celtic tribes which had humbled Rome, some seven hundred years ago. After the enemies' discarded weapons had been destroyed and their own javelins retrieved, he had Marcus arrange the men into a double column for their return to Virulanium. The victorious detachment then made its way south, through the grey-green hinterland, in the almost never-ending drizzle.

On the march back, Versillius spent much time silently considering the justification of what they had just done. The Picts were undoubtedly thieves and raiders and in all likelihood would remain so in the future. But the centurion was now more than ever convinced that they had been punished for crimes, which they had not committed. His new list of suspects pointed towards three people in Virulanium: the legate, the prefect and the governor. One of them was pulling Trajanius' strings. It now seemed more than likely that there there was somebody more senior than the centurion controlling him. So the question that Versillius had yet to answer, was which one of them was the puppet master? The detachment was half way back to the Wall, before Versillius realised that as tedious as it would be, he might be able to put his attendance at the legate's celebratory feast to some use.

Chapter Twenty Two

Maintaining their brisk pace, the men in the column made good time in returning to the fort. The detail arrived back in the middle of the afternoon, in line with the centurion's estimate. Versillius lead them through the north gate, to cheers from the guards in the east and west towers. They were happy to see their comrades returning without any loss or serious injuries. The centurion had Marcus assemble the men on the parade ground and then dismissed them from duty for the rest of the day. On the other side of the barracks, he could hear the sound of new recruits being drilled on the training ground. Were he not about to retire, the centurion would have wandered over to inspect the new intake and see how they were shaping up. But as he was about to leave the army, the centurion knew that he could have little positive impact on their progress. Versillius had a very low opinion of the standard of new recruits, some of whom could barely put together a single sentence in Latin. So instead, he summoned the leader of the daytime watch, Cominius, and briefed him on the results of their mission. The centurion also instructed him to inform the legate, or any other dignitary that asked, about their successful return. Then he returned to his quarters.

After removing his armour and weapons, he put on his civilian clothes and left the barracks. Crossing the forum, the centurion headed straight for the house of pleasure. As it was still daylight, the brothel was locked up and dark on the inside. Versillius thought that Flavala might be shopping in the market place, because there was initially no answer to his thumping on the main entrance. But as he was about to turn away, he heard the sounds of bolts being drawn. In a few more moments, the door opened and he found himself face to face with the proprietor. She stood back in the entrance and after looking him up and down and said, "You were told that you'd get my answer within the week. Not even one day has elapsed since we spoke..."

"Flavala," he replied, "I've just returned from leading a raiding party across the border. I thought you would have heard about my orders and, just possibly, might have been concerned for my safety. The only reason why I am here, is to let you know that I am unharmed and still in one piece."

Still standing back in the darkness, she smiled and responded, "The news about your mission was buzzing around the forum, earlier this morning. And I am pleased to see that you survived, without any injury. But you must forgive me for being so terse with you, there was some trouble here, after you left last night."

"What happened?" he asked, frowning, as this was not something that he was in any way aware of.

"It was caused by two legionnaires from the legate's entourage. They enjoyed the company of my girls and then left without making any payment."

As she spoke, he moved forward and straight away noticed the bruise on her right cheek. A feeling of anger welled up inside him and he said, "They did that to you?"

Flavala nodded and replied, "Well, I could hardly let them leave without making a protest, could I? After all, my women rely on me and if they do not get paid, neither do I."

"Did you hear their names?"

"No, but as I said there were two of them. They also told me that this was the most disgusting establishment that they had ever visited and was far worse than anything to be found in Deva..."

"And the soldier that hit you?" he interjected, "Please describe him to me."

"Versillius, please don't get over protective. Despite my present appearance, I can take care of myself. But if you must know, he was about six inches taller than you and twice as ugly...oh... and he had a beard. But listen, as far as I am concerned it's done now. I am making no official complaint, life and business goes on."

The centurion thought for a moment about the description of her assailant. If the man was six inches taller than him, it would make the soldier around six feet tall. And according to the army's historians, not many soldiers had worn beards since the time of Hadrian. He said, "I'll see what I can do. You may not want the law to help, but I have more than enough men to put the legate's entourage into their place."

"No, Versillius, no!" she replied animatedly, "I don't want you to do a thing. Please, don't put yourself in unnecessary danger. The legate's men will be gone soon and you have such a short time left to serve, that it would be foolish to put your pension at risk. If you still want a favourable answer to your proposal, I suggest that you go to the tavern and calm down."

The centurion was puzzled at her words, because last night she had specifically told him to keep away from Caracalla's bar. Today, she was telling him to go and have a drink. Keeping his confusion to himself, he said, "I'll do as you say. But I also wanted to tell you that I will not be around in the vicus tonight. The prefect's wife has invited me to the grand feast that she is giving, in honour of the legate's visit."

"Well, that should keep you out of trouble, as long as you mind your tongue. Now, go and have a few drinks and forget about my problems, from last night. There is no way that those two men will be allowed to step over the threshold to my establishment again!"

Seeing the resolution in her eyes and hearing the firmness of her voice, Versillius made his farewells and walked the short distance to the tavern. He had wanted to take Flavala in his arms and hold her tightly. But as he was obviously on probation, while she considered his proposal, had decided against it. As he walked into the bar, it was evident that Caracalla was pleased to see one of his best customers returning from a dangerous assignment unharmed. He placed a beer in front of the centurion, as he sat down and said, "This is on the house, my friend. Have this one on me. Any man who protects us from the northern scum deserves a complimentary drink," he then hovered in front of the centurion and continued, somewhat reticently, "But I'm sorry to say that we also need protecting from our own. It was a great pity that you left early last night. I had some trouble with four soldiers from the legate's retinue."

After his conversation with Flavala, Versillius was more than interested to hear what the bar owner had to say. He drained his clay beaker and said to Caracalla, "Tell me, please, what exactly took place?"

"I'll get you a refill first," the owner replied. From behind the bar, he poured another measure of beer into the clay cup and, as he returned to the centurion's table, said, "They came into my tavern, a few minutes after you departed and sat drinking for several hours. Then they got up and left for the house of pleasure without paying for their drinks. I accosted them as they were leaving, but they told me to be quiet, if I knew what was good for me. Although they did promise to settle the slate before returning to Deva."

Versillius was now angry, because this was no way for fellow legionnaires to behave. Firstly, abusing the hospitality of Caracalla and then subsequently two of their number hurting Flavala after refusing to pay her girls for their services. He took a large gulp of his ale and decided that things were now beginning to get personal. Virulanium was his settlement and he had enforced law and order, on both sides of the border, since being a young man. Despite his imminent retirement, the centurion had no intention of allowing this situation to continue or deteriorate. But before he had finished his second beer, the chance to rectify the problem manifested itself. Four armoured and armed soldiers, who he did not recognise, entered the bar. Caracalla visibly shuddered as they walked in, while the centurion noted that only one of them was six feet tall and wearing a bushy beard.

"Four beers, bar owner and be swift about it. We are thirsty after our day's work," one of the shorter men said.

"But you still owe me the money for the drink that you consumed yesterday..." Caracalla replied, somewhat hesitantly.

"I told you last night, man, that we would settle up before returning south. That's the way we do business in our town. But there again, if you do not wish to serve us, then there is an alternative. We could dispense with you and serve ourselves. It would be a great shame to see such a nice tavern damaged, don't you think, men?"

The other three legionnaires, grunted and grinned at the soldier's words. By this stage, Versillius had heard more than he needed to hear. Standing up he stared directly at the ringleader. He was a dark haired man in his mid thirties. Before any of the men could respond, the centurion said, resolutely, "That is enough, legionnaires. I am the centurion for this settlement and will not tolerate such behaviour in Virulanium. However it is you do business in Deva, or any other settlement, those ways do not apply here."

The four soldiers laughed at his words and the tall man with the beard retorted, "You must be old man, Versillius, the centurion who is about to retire. We are not in the least bit scared of you and besides you have no authority over us. The legate is our commanding officer..."

"And civic law and order is still my concern, despite my advanced years. Whether you report to the legate or not you are still subject to Roman law. I could have twenty men here in less than three minutes to haul your sorry arses off to my barracks' jail..."

"The legate would have us out in ten minutes," the shorter man replied, defiantly.

"Possibly," the centurion replied, with menace plainly evident in his voice, "But what exactly would he have released to his care? Your corpses perhaps, because my men can be very careless with their hands...if you get my drift. As I said earlier, you are not in Deva now and there are only four of you. I have nearly eighty of men at my beck and call." The four legionnaires muttered amongst themselves. Suddenly, seeming far less confident, they moved to walk out of the bar.

"Just a moment," Versillius shouted, "You have a debt to settle here and I want to see it paid now. And when you have done that you can go next door and settle the other bill from last night." As they took some coins from their purses he approached the tall, bearded soldier and asked him, "And just who might you be?"

The man glared down at him and said, "I am Nepius Pertinax, second in command to Lucian Fulvius, here, the commander of the general's personal guard."

Versillius assumed that Lucian was the shorter legionnaire, who had done most of the talking. He nodded, before replying, "In this settlement we do not care over much for men who hit women, even if they are members of a legate's bodyguard. You are lucky that Flavala has decided not to press charges against you. But I still have to make up my mind about what will happen to you. Think about that in the course of your stay in Virulanium."

Pertinax grinned at him and said, "What could a short arsed, little cunt like you do against me?"

"Well, I could start by beating you black and blue, just to begin with, before moving onto something more fatal. If you think that your size intimidates me, soldier then you are wrong. Just you pay the money that you owe and leave."

The tall legionnaire smirked at him and answered, "Not even in your wildest dreams, could you best me in personal combat, old man. You would have no chance."

"I killed two Picts today, soldier. And as you work directly for the legate, I doubt that you have ever been into action. Be careful and remember that like myself, all of my men have faced hostile action. But if you fancy your chances against me, then we have a training ground just outside the fort. It is also a place where real soldiers settle their differences with their fists. And I will be there in the morning. Hopefully, so will you."

As the centurion finished addressing Pertinax, who decided not to reply, Lucian threw a handful of coins at Caracalla and the four soldiers left the bar. But rather than being relieved or grateful, the owner turned to him and said, "Bleeding Hades, that was the last thing that I needed you to do tonight, Versillius. They will be back later, after you have gone and they'll smash both me and the tavern to pieces..."

"Give me another beer, please" he replied, "And I have already thought of that possibility. After I have returned to the barracks, there will be a detachment of six armed men, stationed between your tavern and the house of pleasure. They will have strict instructions to arrest the four of them, if they show their faces in this part of the forum. Is that acceptable to you?"

Caracalla nodded, and handed the centurion a top up, which he sank in one long gulp. Putting the stone vessel down, he then left the bar. Outside, dusk was still an hour or so away, but before he could return to the barracks, a visit to the bathhouses was called for. He could hardly turn up at the prefect's formal dinner, looking and smelling like a two day old turd. Then, he realised in an instant, that his visit to the bathhouse might have to be slightly postponed, because waiting for him were the legate's four, troublesome legionnaires. The shorter man, Lucius, addressed him, saying, "Were you serious about facing Pertinax on the training ground? Or was that just an old timer's hot air and wind talking, centurion? We think that now might be a good time."

"I would have preferred to do it tomorrow morning. but give me twenty minutes to find my seconds and you'll find out," Versillius answered, as he stared past Lucius and looked the tall, bearded soldier up and down, with an unflinching intensity in his eyes.

Chapter Twenty Three

The centurion was deadly serious in his resolve to meet the legate's legionnaire on the training ground. But initially, he had to return to the barracks and find Marcus, so that he could act as his second. He also needed to talk to Cominius, the commander of the daytime watch, before the soldier finished his duties for the day. Inside the fort, he encountered Cominius first, as he was stationed on the southern gate. Calling the soldier over, he organised a detachment to stand watch between the tavern and brothel. He explained to the man that the legate's personal bodyguard had caused trouble in the vicus and that night he wanted no re occurrence. The soldier accepted his instructions and promised that he would apprehend the men from Deva, if they caused any more problems. Cominius was already aware of what had taken place on the previous night, in the tavern and house of pleasure. He also promised the centurion that they would not be too gentle, if they had to arrest the legate's soldiers. Feeling reassured by the man's demeanour and attitude, he dismissed him and went to find Marcus.

The young soldier was stretched out on his bed, in the dormitory that he shared with four other soldiers. When he saw his superior officer enter the room, he jumped to his feet and listened attentively as Versillius explained his situation. After digesting the centurion's news, he replied, "I am privileged to be asked to stand as your second, sir. But after our activities across the border, do you think it is wise to face the legate's soldier now?"

"Of course, I did consider that," the centurion answered, "But I laid down the challenge. Even though it took him some time to take it up, I must honour my words. Besides, I think that he is just an obnoxious, streak of piss and no real threat to my well being." Marcus did not respond. But the expression on his face reflected real concern for his superior officer. Versillius recognised this and said, "Stop worrying, I'll be fine. Now come, let us go and get some leather strips from the storeroom. I fear that we are late, already."

After the two men had visited the storeroom, they walked through the east gate and into the training ground. The recruits' drilling session had ended much earlier, so the area was vacant, apart from the four legionnaires from the legate's bodyguard. But soon, there were also a few of Virulanium's soldiers hanging around in groups of two or three. Word of Versillius' challenge had leaked out around the garrison and the soldiers wanted to see how their commander would fare. As Marcus and the centurion approached the men from Deva, Lucius said, "You are late, Versillius! My comrades thought that you had changed your mind and returned to the tavern."

"Well I am here now. If your man, Pertinax, wants to face me, then let us make the preparations," he countered.

The tall soldier was obviously annoyed at being addressed though a third party. He answered, with a distinct tone of irritation in his voice, "I'm more than ready, for you, old man. Stop your talking and get yourself ready for a beating!"

His words and attitude stiffened Versillius in his resolve. Turning away from him, the centurion removed his over garments. Wearing only his *subligaculum* or linen underpants, he extended his arms. Taking the leather strips from the storeroom,

Marcus wrapped them tightly around his fingers and hands. Directly opposite them Pertinax was being made ready in the same fashion. When both soldiers' hands were bound to their satisfaction, their seconds came together. Behind them, the crowd of onlookers had increased in number and included many intrigued citizens, as well as soldiers. Several people were trying to place bets on the outcome of the fight. Most of the money was being placed on the much younger and taller legionnaire, rather than the smaller, but well muscled centurion. Ignoring them, Marcus said to Lucius, "No biting or eye gouging, otherwise anything else is permitted. Are we in agreement?"

"We have no problem with those rules. But I do suggest that you summon this settlement's physician to tend to your centurion, for when Nepius Pertinax has finished pounding him!"

"I'll consider summoning the physician when the fight is over," Marcus countered, "That is, when I have seen who requires his services." The young soldier then turned his back on Lucius and returned to his superior officer. He explained that the opponent's second had agreed the terms and said, "Best of luck, sir. Give him a good one or two for me."

Marcus then stood to one side and the two combatants advanced to meet each other. The crowd, which had now grown to quite a size, let out a collective gasp of expectation. Pertinax took the lead, rushing quickly at the smaller man, with his long arms outstretched. Versillius maintained his slow walk towards his adversary, keeping calm and focused. As the taller man bore down swiftly on him, he tried to grab the centurion's shoulders. Versillius waited until the last moment and ducked underneath his grasp. Then aiming his right shoulder towards Pertinax's chest, he took the full impact of the man's charge.

Both men fell to the ground, but Versillius was the first to his feet. Pertinax had been badly winded by the centurion's manoeuvre. As he stood up, the tall legionnaire caught his breath and said, "A neat trick, old timer. But is that the best that you can do?"

The two men were now stood less than a yard apart. Versillius decided that it was time for him to make a move. Rather recklessly, he threw a strong right hand punch at his opponent. As the blow missed, he knew instantly that he had made a bad mistake. The momentum of the blow had carried him towards Pertinax. The tall soldier had seen the punch coming and dodged it easily. He also saw that the centurion had dropped his left hand guard, and taking his opportunity counter punched with own his left hand. Versillius tried to avoid the blow, but could not get out of its way and the punch connected with his right eye. Stunned by the force of the impact, the centurion instinctively moved forwards and clasped the other man, around his torso. The crowd started to boo and whistle, as the two fighters went into a clinch. But that didn't concern Versillius, he just needed a few seconds for his head to clear. Pertinax, now feeling certain that he had the upper hand, pushed him off and said, "There's more waiting for you, a lot more than that. Now, why don't you try to fight like a man, rather than an old woman?"

Versillius suddenly looked very worried and backed away from his opponent. But this time when Pertinax advanced, he held up his guard and threw no reckless punches. Instead, he absorbed the soldier's combination on his arms and then as the blows subsided, jabbed with his left hand. It connected beautifully with the tall legionnaire's bearded chin. Pertinax's forward movement had carried him onto the jab. For a moment, he was defenceless, as his legs buckled. Taking advantage of his opponent's incapacity, Versillius crashed his right hand into the man's stomach. Pertinax groaned and staggered backwards, desperately trying to raise his guard. But the smaller man was much quicker and this time his right hand to the head found its mark. The punch landed on the soldier's temple, stunning him completely. By now, Pertinax had his arms by his side. Wanting to finish the, fight before sustaining any further injuries, Versillius planted a fearsome, left uppercut into his now defenceless opponent's testicles. That heavy punch would have felled a wild bull, let alone a human being. As it landed, the taller legionnaire let out a strange, high pitched squealing noise, the like of which had never been heard before in Virulanium. He then slowly sank to his knees, before collapsing on the ground.

    The centurion then walked back to Marcus, as the defeated man's comrades came to tend to him. In the background, the crowd cheered wildly, even Vespasianus and Paribius. Their own man, the centurion from Virulanium, their settlement, had beaten a taller and much younger opponent. As he approached Marcus, the younger soldier warmly embraced him and said, with the elation in his voice obvious, "Well done, sir. You had me worried until you backed away. That's when I knew that you had him beaten. I doubt there's a better counter puncher than you on the whole of the northern frontier..."

Chapter Twenty Four

After picking up his clothes and leaving the training ground behind him, the centurion went straight to the public baths. He had a quick dip in the *tepiderium* and an even faster steam in the calderium. Then Versillius returned to the barracks. There he put on his smartest, formal garments; a cream toga, an unstained tunica and his cleanest trousers. While dressing, Versillius considered the black eye that Pertinax had given him. No doubt, several of Gaius Flavius' dinner guests would have something to say about that. But unlike his outward demeanour, there was nothing he could do to change his facial appearance. He then made the short walk to the western vicus and the prefect's villa. This took him through the ornately decorated west gate, which was not yet locked, as the sun had only just gone down.

The same slave, whom he had seen two nights ago, greeted him at the prefect's door. The man led him into the dining area, where the guests were already fully reclined on the softly padded couches. It was a large room, whose plastered walls were mainly painted in a pastel, lime green colour. There were also several decorative frescoes; large panels depicting the activities of Neptune, Venus and Mars. To his surprise he saw that Drusilla, the high priestess, was amongst the guests. She looked resplendent, as she was wearing her best golden jewellery and was reclining proudly, between the legate and the governor. There were also two other men present, strangers that he had not seen before. As he walked towards the sole vacant couch, the prefect's wife Juliana said, "Versillius, it is such a pleasure to see you here tonight. When you last visited my home, it was so late in the night that I was unable to greet you. But I was beginning to be afraid that your duties might have detained you, this evening. I was just about to serve the food to our guests. Now, I don't think that you know Aulus Falerius and Tertius Plinius. They are merchants, who have accompanied the legate, all the way from Deva."

Juliana was a plain woman, in her early fifties. When standing, she was at least two inches taller than her husband. Unlike the flamboyant priestess, her jewellery was made of silver and ivory pins secured her greying hair. But her strong personality more than made up for her lack of good looks. Although the prefect often made her out to be some kind of dragon, Versillius had never encountered anything but kindness and friendship from Juliana, in the twenty years that he had known her. As far as he was aware, the only real strain on their marriage had been when their son had been killed, fighting with the legions in Germania. That was roughly around the same time that Gaius Flavius had started to lose his temper with everybody on a regular basis. Putting those thoughts out of his mind, the centurion reclined on the empty couch, on his left hand side, in the same manner as the other guests. He nodded to the two merchants, and the two men returned his greeting, before Aulus Falerius said, "The legate promised us an introduction to your man Vespasianus. It seems that nothing shifts in Virulanium without his say so."

Realising that the statement required no answer, Versillius smiled and then turned to his hostess and said, "Forgive my late appearance, but I also had business to attend to on this side of the border. Juliana, let me thank you for your kind invitation, it was..."

But before he could finish, the legate propped himself up on one elbow and interrupted, "Business across the border, which was not completed, as I understand it. Your soldiers tell me that you didn't burn down the Picts' village, let alone countenance slaughtering their women and children. After all your years of service, centurion, I would have expected you to know the true meaning of a reprisal raid."

"We killed over twenty Scots, legate, in the course of the battle. It is my opinion that was sufficient punishment, anything else would have been as barbaric as they are. Such a small settlement will find it very hard to recover from that level of loss."

The legate shrugged and reclined again before replying, "And then there is also the matter of you threatening my men in the tavern this afternoon. The priestess tells me that the bar is well known as your second home. In my view, your language and conduct was totally unjustified. I expect my legion's soldiers to be treated with respect, while they are visiting this dismal settlement."

"If they choose to defraud our traders and use violence against women, then my language and conduct was more than totally justified," the centurion retorted.

"He could be right," the governor, Quintus Lucius cut in, as always rather nervously, "I did hear that your bodyguards had behaved rather badly in the vicus last night."

Appius Severus looked at him contemptuously and said, in the manner of a man addressing a small and simple minded child, "My soldiers will be warriors, which is what I want them to be. If they were anything else, other than aggressive, then they would end up being incapable of fighting. They would be no better than the so called legionnaires of this garrison, who seem to be unable to carry out the simplest massacre of defeated Picts. But you have all not yet heard the full extent of this centurion's behaviour. Tell me, prefect, were you aware that he had a pitched brawl with one of my legionnaires on the training ground?"

Gaius Flavius obviously had not yet heard this news. But the centurion's black eye attested to its verity. He turned to his centurion and said, defiantly, "I'll talk to you about that later, Versillius. And if you didn't emerge as the victor then you will be in a great deal of trouble! I would hate the legate to feel that the legionnaires in Virulanium were unable to fight and beat another soldier, after a mere five hours of forced march and battle!"

As the prefect finished, the legate raised his eyebrows at the senior official's response. But before he could reply, Drusilla cut in saying, "It is my view, that the men at this fort seem far more interested in brawling and accusing innocent people of murder, rather than doing their job correctly. We pay our taxes for protection from the Picts and we are not getting value for our money!"

The centurion replied to her words, by saying, through tightly, clenched teeth,"Priestess, I have decided to eliminate you from any suspicion in the death of Antonius, following the murder of Paribius. I would have told you earlier, but the legate had other duties for me to perform today."

His reply received no acknowledgement from Drusilla, as the priestess ignored his words completely. Instead, she turned towards to the legate and said to him in an audible whisper, "When this officer retires, I'd be grateful if he could be replaced with somebody more competent. And I dare say that the gods would also be very appreciative, as well! This town needs a younger centurion who respects and worships the old deities, in the same way that you do, Appius Severus." As she spoke, her right hand playfully caressed the legate's thigh.

The patrician legate smiled at her words and touch before replying, "They have nurtured and protected Rome for over eight hundred years and I constantly pray for their guidance. But in my opinion there should never have been a murder enquiry mounted in the first place. I knew within a few minutes of arriving in Virulanium that this was the work of the Picts. Anybody who possessed even half a brain would have seen that." He then glanced at the centurion as he finished talking. Meanwhile, Drusilla's right hand had slipped underneath the legate's toga. A stern glance in her direction, from Juliana, caused it to be withdrawn immediately. It was not that sort of a feast. The general went on to to say, "But once we get new blood in positions of authority, this place should pick up!"

That was it. After the battle with the Picts and his fight with Pertinax, Versillius had now heard more than he could stomach. Especially from such an arrogant man and a stupid priestess, both of whom he personally despised. Keeping his emotions under control, he made to rise slowly from his couch and depart, but before he could do so the prefect's wife stated loudly, "I have two rules in this house, when we are entertaining guests, which I hope you will all obey. The first is that you may talk about politics and religion as much as you like. But you must leave your official business until the morning. And my second rule is that the conversation must not be personal. Now, Versillius, I insist that you make yourself comfortable and relax. Look, the servants are bringing in the first course, as I speak."

Both the general and the centurion were left with no choice but to heed Juliana's words, given the stern tone of her voice. The prefect broke the silence, and tried to lighten the atmosphere by saying, "I'm afraid that we can't run to the normal twenty courses these days. You just can't get the provisions from the continent any longer. But I can promise you a good twelve servings. And as a special treat, I've raided my wine cellar in your honour, legate. We shall drink fine red wine with our food tonight!"

Looking less than impressed, Appius Severus rolled his eyeballs at the ceiling and said, "I would have expected nothing less from you, Gaius Flavius. When you are entertaining me, I expect to be served the finest food and wine that is available. After all, it is not every day that I travel this far north," He then looked at the priestess and continued, "Perhaps, dear lady, you would be gracious enough to say a few words to the deities, before we start? Somebody needs to thank them for providing us with these morsels of food and drink." In defiance of his hostess, his hand then reached across and stroked the priestess' upper, inner thigh.

Drusilla needed no second bidding, from such a high-ranking person, who was so obviously responsive to her sexual overtures. She immediately launched into a lengthy prayer to Jupiter, as the servants brought in the first dish and a large amphora filled with red wine. At her husband's side Juliana managed to keep her emotions under control. But the centurion could see that she was seething inside, at the legate's overt behaviour with the priestess and his haughty, dismissive attitude of her efforts. Versillius knew that she must have gone to a great deal of trouble and expense to prepare a twelve-course feast, for eight people, in just one day. When the Drussilla finally finished her prayer, one of the two travelling merchants, Aulus Falerius said, "I must say that it's not too easy to get hold of things these days. My colleague and I have travelled north with only pottery and glassware to sell. You can't get good olive oil or decent red wine in Londinium or Eboracum for neither love or money."

Chapter Twenty Five

At around the same time that the prefect's guests were about to be served their first course, another ritual was getting under way. Unlike the feast, this gathering was not taking place in the comfort of a heated villa. Beyond the far eastern side of the vicus, a long walk away from the training ground, was a grassy hollow. It was sheltered from both the fort and the via east by a small forest of pine trees. The garrison harvested these when they were needed to repair the internal fabric of the fort's buildings or its fixtures. On a tree felling detail some months ago, Trajanius had seen the location and decided that it was the ideal place to establish Virulanium's temple of Mithras. Out of sight from his superiors and any casual passer by, it offered the opportunity for his small band of followers to worship their god. As their meetings were held after the sun had set, the enclosed hollow had the feel of being a dark underground chamber, like the more established temples along the Wall.

But this *Mithraeum* had its disadvantages, being as it was just a depression surrounded by trees and grassy banks. Despite the legionnaire's energetic recruitment drive, so far he had only three followers, all fellow comrades. And until their number rose, the religion lacked the funds to build a walled, roofed and underground structure. But he told himself that would soon change and once the money was raised they would have a temple to rival the building in *Brocolitia*. His optimism was not entirely unfounded, because the reason for that night's gathering was the initiation of a fourth recruit. Caletus, a young probationary legionnaire, would soon attain the lowest rank of *corax*, or raven. That was if he could come through the stringent ordeal tests, which a would be follower had to pass.

In preparation for this occasion, Caletus had been stripped to his undergarments. He was now standing in the trees, with the other three legionnaires, where he had been for some time. This was the ordeal of cold. It required an aspirant to subject his uncovered body to the elements for an hour. While the potential novitiate underwent the first test, Trajanius had prepared his "temple" for the full initiation ceremony. Firstly, he had lit a wooden fire. As it was dark, the smoke would not be seen from the fort and the flames were hidden by the trees. He had then placed a wooden board, which was his portable altar, at one end of the knoll. Onto this, he had reverently secured three small, but rudely carved images. The first showed Mithras bursting from the cosmic egg, ready to start his search for the primeval bull. At his side were his faithful attendants: *Cautes*, whose upturned torch represented sunrise and *Cautophates*, whose down turned torch represented sunset.

When the fire was glowing brightly, the legionnaire placed the mask of a heliotrope on his face. This was also fashioned out of wood, in the shape of a glowing sun. Pulling his paenula cloak around himself, as the night air was chilly, Trajanius smiled. Caletus had almost finished his time in the woods. If he had successfully completed the first stage, it was time to summon him to the "temple". The legionnaire walked away from the fire, up a bank and into a copse. Just inside the trees he saw the four men. Silius Bolanus was the senior of his three followers. He had obtained the rank of *perses* or persian. His mask was bearded and topped with the distinct eastern headgear. Trajanius said to him, "Has our would be brother passed his first test?"

"Yes, heliodromus," was his terse reply. The other two men, Capiton and Hiberus, who were a level lower than Silius Bolanus, confirmed this. Their rank was that of *leo* or lion. Caletus, the aspirant, shivered as Trajanius stated, "Then bring the would be brother into our temple. It is time for him to face the next test."

The heliodromus led the way, as the three legionnaires escorted Caletus down the bank. Trajanius stood waiting, in front of the four men and gestured towards the fire saying, "The ordeal of facing cold has been accomplished. But our lord Mithras was faced with more than one test, before he attained true worthiness!" Moving towards the almost naked, young man, he continued, "It is now time for you to face ordeal by fire. Place your back close to the flames while I count to one hundred. If you move away, then you will have failed the rite and you cannot go onto the next level. Our religion will be closed to you forever. Is that understood?"

Caletus, whose teeth were chattering, was unable to utter a sound in reply. Instead, he nodded his head and staggered across to the fire. Placing his back against the heat, he waited for Trajanius to start counting. As the heliodromus commenced the count, the probationary legionnaire initially felt relief from the cold. but as the numbers reached double figures, this feeling vanished and was replaced with one of intense pain. The pain turned into agony as the counting reached the half way stage. He gritted his teeth, having resolved to see the ordeals through. A young and impressionable man, Caletus did not want to lose face in front of the older comrades that he respected. After what seemed like forever, Trajanius finished counting and gestured for him to move away from the flames. He needed no second bidding and threw himself forward, onto the cold, damp ground. Allowing him no time to recover, Trajanius asked, "Has this miserable wretch taken food or drink in the course of today?"

Silius Bolanus, the persian, replied, "I watched him closely from sunrise, along with my two other brothers. At no time did we see anything pass his mouth."

"Does your brother speak the truth?" Trajanius asked Caletus.

"He does, heliodromus," the soldier gasped back in reply, as his body cooled down. The sun masked figure nodded intently and went onto say, "Now there are only two more levels for you to negotiate. Obedience and your vows of loyalty. We will start with obedience..." As his words tailed off, the persian handed Trajanius a rod. The heliodromus swished it in the air, around his head and then brought it down on the aspirant's shoulders. It was a stinging blow, which caused Caletus great pain, but the young legionnaire withheld his cry of pain, as Trajanius asked him, "What do we say to that, soldier?"

"Give me...give me another, please...heliodromus..."

Again the rod came crashing down and the process was repeated several more times, until Trajanius was satisfied that the ordeal was completed. When he was finished, the other three men had to help Caletus to his feet. As they supported him, Trajanius placed the rod on the ground and said, "It is now time to take our vows. Tell me brothers, who do we pledge ourselves to, even unto the point of death?"

"Mithras," all four men replied, the initiate Caletus somewhat groggily.

"And who do we serve in this world?"

"Magnentius, our great emperor. We offer him our loyalty without any qualification!"

"Who else do we pledge our allegiance to?" Trajanius continued his arms now outstretched.

"The pater, who looks after us, on behalf of the emperor and Mithras," was their joint response. Their answers were correct and satisfied the self appointed runner of the sun. Addressing Caletus, he said, "You have done well, brother. I am pleased to award you the rank of corax. Fashion yourself a mask in the shape of the raven, before our next meeting. But now it is time for you to approach the altar and give thanks to Mithras. Without his intercession, you would not have come through these ordeals!"

The other legionnaires released their latest recruit, who stumbled towards the altar. Whether he prostrated himself in front of Mithras or fell over, was unclear. But as he offered homage to the deity, Silius Bolanus said to Trajanius, "Where is the pater? You promised us that he would be here tonight. Do you think that we are prepared to put up with this shambles forever?"

Trajanius, swallowed nervously and answered rather awkwardly, "The pater is always with us. But everything must come together before he can make himself known. Have patience, brother perses, the time is almost upon us..."

"It better had be, for your sake," Capiton interjected, "You promised us all wealth and advancement if we followed your leadership. So far all we have received is a severe beating and a roasting!"

The slightly built legionnaire swallowed very heavily this time, while retrieving his altar and miniature images. Before heading back to the barracks alone, he said confidently, "Have faith, my brothers. I am more than sure that our pater will see that we are all rewarded for our loyalty and devotion."

He did nor hear Silius Bolanus muttering loudly to himself, "My fucking arse!"

Chapter Twenty Six

Meanwhile, inside the prefect's villa, the servants had served the first course. The starter was sauteed, chopped leeks, which were served with bread and a large bowl of olive oil. The smell of the food pleasantly assailed Versillius, as he realised that it was now over twenty-four hours since he had last eaten. That had been when he was in the forum with Marcus, while they were waiting for Paribius to return to his shop. The centurion was even more pleased to the see the bowl of olive oil, something that he had not tasted for several months. He resolved to get his share and looked forward to his toilet being a little easier in the morning. Reaching forwards, he dipped some of the bread into the green liquid and after letting it soak for a few moments, devoured it. Then taking two handfuls of the leeks, he looked on with pleasure as the servants filled his opaque blue glass with red wine, from clay jugs that they had submersed in the amphora. After finishing the leeks, he drained the first glass of wine in one gulp. Unlike the beverage Flavala had given him the previous night, this was not stale and he relished the taste. Even better, as he replaced his glass at his side, it was instantly topped up, by one of the prefect's servants.

The next course was a large dish of wild blackberries, to cleanse the palate. In earlier times, this would have been black olives. But as the prefect pointed out to his guests, such commodities were not seen this far north, at the present time. The two merchants echoed his sentiments, with doleful expressions on their faces. Before the third course was brought in, Gaius Flavius rose to his feet and said, "As a tribute to our noble visitor, Appius Severus, we will now have a very special third starter. My dear wife had to search long and hard in the market place for this delicacy. But she was able to locate enough of the little beasts, so that we can now enjoy the rare treat of door mice, stuffed with ground wheat and garlic."

The large plate was placed before them and Versillius picked up one of the tiny roasted animals. They were not greatly to his taste. But out of politeness to Juliana, he removed two small strips of flesh from its chest, which took less than one mouthful to dispose of. He then discarded the stuffed body. Appius Severus who was now dropping morsels of door mice into Drusilla's all too eager mouth also seemed under impressed by the dish, saying, "What's next prefect, larks' tongues?"

Gaius Flavius replied, "There might have been, legate, if you had given me more notice of your visit. Those little birds take time to catch. But there is another great delicacy for your taste buds to savour. Our next course is grilled char from the lake land area, bought fresh from the market, today."

Several of the guests, Versillius included, licked their lips in anticipation, as the servants brought the dish into the centre of the room. The char was not unlike a trout, but had been specially imported from Italia, by the early Roman settlers. It was bred exclusively in the cold water of the northern lakes, on the western side of the Wall. The centurion tucked into a portion of the pink fish enjoying its rich flavour, far more than the paltry bits of meat from the door mouse. There was then a short break, while their glasses were topped up, before the next dish was served. While they let the first four courses settle, the governor turned to Appius Severus and said, "The rumours say that you will not be in our presence for much longer, now that we have a new emperor, Magnentius, on the throne. I must say that you will be sorely missed, legate."

As Versillius nearly choked on his wine at the governor's words, Appius Severus replied, "If I am summoned to return to the imperial city, then as a soldier, I must obey orders. There are rumours that our new emperor plans a campaign of conquests and may have need of men of my calibre. Although, I will say, that it had been my hope to leave the twentieth legion in much better shape than it is today. Perhaps my successor will have the chance to rectify this failure on my part, now that there is new blood being recruited and old soldiers due to retire." And after several glasses of wine Drusilla seemed less awed by her hostess, as her hand again furtively slipped under the legate's toga.

The centurion knew that the general's final comment was aimed directly at him, but refused to rise to the bait. He sipped on his wine, as the servants brought in the fifth course, a selection of roasted vegetables. Versillius only took a small portion from the dish of mixed beetroot, swede and turnip. The centurion wanted to save some room in his stomach for the meat courses, which he knew would be served next. After they had finished eating the roasted vegetables, the prefect said to Appius Severus, "But is there any point in going back to Rome, legate? From what I have read in official despatches, the centre of government has shifted east, to Constantinople. Surely, you'd be better off staying here?"

The legate grimaced and responded, "I was born in Rome. People like you, who were born on this damp, miserable island and have never seen the imperial city, cannot conceive of its splendour and glory. At times I seriously wonder why the emperor

Claudius ever bothered to conquer this wet place. Rest assured, if I was summoned to Rome at this very moment, then I would pack and go there immediately."

As he finished, Drusilla withdrew her hand from the general's toga and said, "The former emperor Constantine has a lot to answer for, a great deal more than Claudius, in my opinion. Not only did he move the empire's capital to the east, he also tried to prevent the worship of the ancient deities. It is no wonder that we are now on hard times, when we are told to worship the Christian god. You will find no image of Constantine in my temple."

Apart from those images on the coins given to you as tribute, Versillius thought to himself, as he yet again held his tongue.

"Personally, I have no doubt that the man was a complete idiot," the legate stated, draining his glass of wine and then reaching across to fondle the priestesses' firm breasts, "He abolished crucifixion and tried to do the same with gladiatorial combat. What would great warriors and leaders like Julius Caesar or Tiberius make of that? I ask you all, how can we hope to deter criminals without having the proper forms of punishment available to us for retribution under the law?"

Before anybody could reply, or Juliana express her displeasure at his behaviour, the servants re-entered the room. They were carrying a side of roasted boar, on a salver. The prefect made a sigh of anticipation and took up his carving knife and fork. While the official sliced the meat, Juliana said to Versillius, "Have you decided what you are going to do, after your retirement?"

"Not really," he replied, "My main priority is to settle into the villa. Perhaps when that is done, and

I've adjusted to civilian life, I'll see what opportunities that there are."

She smiled at him, saying, "I'm sure that I speak for my husband, when I say that if you need our assistance in any way, then you only need to ask."

He thanked her kindly for the offer and took a slice of the carved wild boar. It tasted very succulent and was cooked to perfection. But still, the centurion did not overburden his stomach, as there were more dishes to be served. The next arrived in a few minutes, chunks of beef, which had been casseroled in a red wine and garlic sauce. Using the pointed end of his spoon, he took several pieces of meat from the embossed samian bowl and placed them on his silver plate. Versillius then reversed the spoon and covered the meat with the pungent sauce. As he ate, the legate stated firmly, "As I was saying, prefect, I have no doubt that Rome will reassert its position. After all, we are a society that is over eight hundred years old, with the largest empire that the world has ever seen. This fixation with the east has lasted for barely more than one hundred years." Drusilla's hand gently stroked his cheek, as he spoke.

"I sincerely hope so," the second merchant, Tertius Plinius interrupted, "An honest man can barely make a living now that everything is sent to the east. I can't remember the last time that we had a vessel dock with produce from the warmer parts of the empire."

Gaius Flavius did not reply, but the governor twitched his assent at these words. The conversation then halted, because the servants had returned, with the eighth course, thin strips of barbecued lamb. The centurion thought that the prefect looked totally unconvinced at the logic of the legate's argument, as he helped himself to the meat. Versillius was starting to feel quite full now, so he just ate one strip, which he washed down with a swig of red wine. But the next course had him reaching for his spoon, because it was wild mushrooms steamed in milk and herbs, a particular favourite of his. Mercifully, there was a break before the tenth course, a selection of cow and goat cheeses. The centurion glanced across at Juliana and said, "Although the cheese looks very enticing, I must pass. My stomach is now in grave danger of splitting both my trousers and tunica."

"My belly feels the same as yours Versillius, I think that I've rather overdone things," the prefect cut in, "So if nobody minds, I'm going to pay a quick visit to the *vomitarium* and empty my tummy, as I intend to enjoy the rest of this meal. You are more than welcome to accompany me, centurion. I'd hate to see the cheese going to waste."

As he rose from his couch and left the room, Versillius shook his head, saying, "I'm full, prefect, but not quite full enough to keep you company."

"I think that you overdid the wild mushrooms, centurion. They have always been a favourite of yours, haven't they?" Juliana stated, with a smile, as she took up several slices of cheese and a piece of bread.

"It's more likely that he overdid the red wine," Appius Severus muttered to Drusilla, who smiled. The prefect's wife overheard the comment and replied, "You will remember my two rules, when I am entertaining you as a guest."

The legate bowed his head, as a gesture of respect to his hostess and returned to his portion of cheese. Versillius also had to pass on the next course, a selection of fruits. There were apples, pears, dried figs and dates, the latter two coming from the prefect's private cellar. Shortly after the prefect returned from the vomitarium, the legate and Drusilla decided that they needed to visit the vomitarium together. It was so obvious what they were going to do there that even Versillius cringed at their brazen behaviour. While they were away, the guests chatted awkwardly, making small talk. After some fifteen minutes the pair returned, both looking quite flushed and perspiring heavily. After they had reclined on their couches, the servants were able to serve the final course. It was an individual selection of sweetmeats, intricately decorated and coloured dainties. They were made from flour and the stewed residue of the sugar beet and coated with honey. Underneath them, there was a message, from the hosts, written on a small piece of vellum. This usually caused a great deal of amusement to the assembled guests. Normally, they would take it in turns to read each one out, not knowing whether it would be sentimental or sarcastic. The legate seemed to think that his message was of the latter type, as it read *Look to the north, dear friend. We need you here.*

    Taking exception to its contents, he first crumpled and then dropped the small piece of parchment to the floor. Without sharing the text, with his fellow guests, he rose to his feet said abruptly, "I thank you for your hospitality, Juliana and Gaius Flavius, but I have had a long day. Come, Quintus Lucius, it is time for us to go."

    The prefect had already been told that the legate would be staying the night at the governor's villa, which was only a short distance away. The governor had several residences in the vicii along the Wall. But his villa in Virulanium was reputed to be his favourite. Quintus Lucius hurriedly rose from the dining couch and bidding his fellow diners farewell, made ready to leave the room. Drusilla also prepared to depart, as the legate said to her, "We will speak again in the morning, priestess, at the temple. Remember that my audit and census has been ordered by the emperor Magnentius."

"As a true believer, you are guaranteed not only my fullest co-operation but also that of the gods," she replied, fervently, making a gesture of deference. No doubt similar to the one she had made in the vomitarium, Versillius thought to himself.

"I thank you again, Juliana," Appius Severus said to his hostess as he departed, which Quintus Lucius and Drusilla endorsed, before they followed him out of the dining area. The legate then momentarily reappeared and retrieved his crumpled message from the floor. Before addressing the prefect, he flicked the ball of parchment at him and said, "Gaius Flavius, remember that although every body laughs at a fool, nobody actually wants one. Especially not as their chief administrator..."

Chapter Twenty Seven

That left just the centurion and the two merchants, in the company of the prefect and his wife. The two traders swiftly rose to their feet, as they were also due to spend the night at the governor's villa. They thanked Juliana profusely for her hospitality and made themselves ready to leave. The second merchant, Tertius Plinius, asked Versillius if it was possible to meet him the following day. He wanted to see if the centurion needed to order any pots or glassware for his impending retirement. His offer was respectfully, but firmly declined. When the itinerant traders had departed, the prefect turned to his wife and tried to make light of the legate's insult and saying, "That was a strange end to the evening, I can only assume that Appius Severus took exception to his message. I only wrote it to humour him. Honestly, the man has an even worse disposition than I do, myself. Never mind, my dear, at least we've done our duty and more besides."

"It's absolutely beyond me that why you refuse to make an official complaint to the proconsul in Eboracum about that man. It's not the first time that he has insulted you, in your own home, and behaved towards the both of us in a despicable way!" was Juliana's agitated reply.

The prefect shuddered at her words and said, "Calm down, my dear. I can see that you are tired, after all the work that you have put into preparing the feast..."

"Don't you even try to and pacify me," she interjected, "I'm not pleased, Gaius Flavius, not in the slightest. The man insulted you in front of our guests. He was also pretty beastly to Versillius. And then he fucked that old whore, who pretends to be a priestess, in our vomitarium. It's all very well for him to move up and down the Wall and then back to Deva, with his crowd of hangers on. All he does is scrounge off people like ourselves, living for free and at no cost to himself whatsoever! His only ambition is to return to Rome and he constantly denigrates our settlement and hospitality. Do you actually have any idea at all, just how much this feast set us back?"

"Please, not now dear, we do still have one guest present. I'm sure that you're making him feel very awkward..."

"I'm sorry, Versillius," she responded, turning to the centurion and grasping his right hand, said, "Please believe me, that I do not begrudge you a single mouthful of food or the smallest sip of wine. It's just that I cannot abide that arrogant, patrician phallus! He believes that because he was born in Rome, that he is somehow better than we are. Well he's not. In my opinion he's just a pompous, overbearing, rude bag of shit! I also hope that slut of a priestess was able to keep her subligaculum from dropping around her ankles on her way home! Now there, I've had my say. And as it's all off my chest, I'll leave you two men alone to finish the jug of wine. I wish you both a good night."

The prefect smiled, as she left the room, and refilled their glasses, saying, "Versillius, now that I have broken the seal on the last amphora there seems little sense in allowing the wine to go stale. I do hope you'll stay for a while and help me finish it. And by the way, let me congratulate you on your victory over the general's bodyguard. It's good to take that lot down a peg or two and show them that we are not all country cousins."

"I couldn't agree with you more," the centurion replied, taking a sip of the red liquid, "And I'll stay as long as you like, provided you tell me just what's on your mind, Gaius Flavius."

"You are a very perceptive fellow, Versillius. I take back everything that I've ever said and anything that I will probably say against you, in the future. Er...it's probably nothing to worry about, but I do feel in need of your advice. Since Antonius was murdered, I've had nobody to bounce ideas off..." His voice tailed off and he paced around the couches before resuming, "Today, when you were across the border, the legate came to me and demanded the keys to the treasury. He wanted to could carry out his audit in private. I refused, of course, as I have still received no official notification of the census from Eboracum. But he said that our late chief scribe had been informed and that must have been one of the communications that Antonius had either lost or misplaced. I'm sure that you realise that it puts me in a very awkward position."

The prefect had always been a more than just a dedicated public servant. He had personally followed every law to the limit of each letter that it contained. But unlike the pedantic Antonius, when dealing with the settlement, he had also applied the spirit as well as the letter of the law. This approach had benefited many citizens, who might other wise have been placed at a disadvantage. The concept of *civitas*, or pride in serving the community, might have been invented to describe him. His entire career had been spent in the service of Virulanium and several other settlements along the Wall. Despite their frequent disagreements, Versillius had nothing but total respect for the way that the man carried out his duties. "Do you suspect something?" the centurion asked, his own suspicions more than aroused.

"Of course not, but rules are rules. I agreed with him that we would inspect the treasury tomorrow, in your company, once he had finished his audit of the temple. Despite his high rank, I can't go handing out the keys to the treasury, without the correct documentation. As we no longer get any coins from Rome, our settlement's entire wealth and economic well being is stored there. If you don't mind, could you meet me in the civic buildings tomorrow morning, after you have bathed?"

"Of course, I shall be happy to help. But let me ask you something, prefect. I'm afraid it is of a delicate nature, like the door mice we consumed earlier."

"Feel free to go ahead," the official replied, with a puzzled look on his face.

"Thank you," Versillius replied, "There is something happening in Virulanium, which I have not yet got to the bottom of. Are you aware of the revival of Mithraism that is currently taking place?"

"Well your man Trajanius, tried to recruit me, but that's as much as I know about it," the prefect answered.

"So you are not the pater to his heliodromus?" the centurion asked.

"Versillius, I do believe that you are interrogating me. As for Trajanius and his silly rituals, that's for you to resolve. But you are going to assist me tomorrow, aren't you?"

Versillius was happy to agree and after thanking the prefect for his hospitality and confidence, decided that it was time to return to the barracks. He even declined a further glass of wine from the official, as he wanted to keep a relatively clear head to think about the prefect's words. But before he could leave Gaius Flavius said to him, "With the legate's sudden and abrupt departure, you didn't get a chance to read the message under your sweat meat. Juliana composed it for you. So please, read it out for me."

"Only if you give me the glass of wine, which I refused a few moments ago," Versillius answered, being unable to resist his own, hedonistic urges. While his glass was being refilled, the centurion picked up the small piece of parchment which read, *Eat your sweetmeat but marry your sweetheart*.

The white haired prefect grinned and said to him, "My wife heard about your proposal in the forum, when she was shopping for the feast. You know how gossip swiftly travels around our settlement. In my opinion, Flavala will be very good for you, Versillius. As well as being a very attractive woman she's also very good at business matters. Bear in mind, that you'll need something to do, to occupy your time, when you leave the army, as my wife was saying earlier. Now, finish your wine, so that I can bid you a good night."

"Before I go, may I ask what did your message was, Gaius Flavius?"

"Oh, just a little ditty from my wife," he replied, laughing nervously, as he read out the words on his tiny piece of vellum, "*Married men have their own house of pleasure and need no other!* It is one of Juliana's little jokes...I think."

"And the governor's message, what did Juliana write for him?"

The prefect grinned and not bothering to retrieve the slip said, "If I had been writing the message, it would have read, *Ask the legate for your balls back.* But I have no idea what my wife finally composed for him...and no real interest either"

Chapter Twenty Eight

The chilly, night air soon brought the centurion to his senses, as he walked away from the prefect's villa, towards the southern gate. He had quite enjoyed the feast, despite the company of the legate and the ominous presence of Drusilla. But their sexual antics and act of coupling in the vomitarium would present him and the settlement with great amusement for many a day. With his stomach also full of olive oil and red wine, Versillius knew that he would sleep well from the latter. He also hoped that the former would allow him to complete his motions easily the following day. However, his journey back to the barracks was interrupted before he even reached the locked western wall. The centurion was just leaving the area where the villas were located, when two men emerged from behind some bushes and lunged violently at him. In the light of the moon he could see that they were wearing rough trousers and blue body paint. He could also see that their faces were darkened. His feelings of satisfaction and well being disappeared swiftly, as the centurion saw that they were pointing long bladed spathae at him. Their swords were then thrust towards him several times. Versillius managed to dodge the blows, moving backwards swiftly. Without saying a word, the two men stayed their thrusts momentarily, but then resumed their advance towards him. In the face of their menacing movements, he continued to retreat.

Versillius was both startled and confused. The men were obviously Picts, but their sword thrusts were Roman. But he had no time to consider the finer points of this logic, as they were almost upon him. Although he did not have his own gladius dangling from his belt, in light of the recent murders he had taken precautions. Before leaving the barracks, he had strapped his sheathed pugio around his right ankle, underneath his right trousers' leg. In one swift movement, the centurion bent down and drew the blade with his right hand. His assailants momentarily backed off, seeing the glint of the iron, in the light of the moon. Still speechless, they glanced at each other, and having seen the shortness of the centurion's knife, continued their advance. But Versillius still had a trick left up his sleeve. While he had been removing his dagger, with his right hand, he had gathered up a handful of soil with his other hand. As the two men came onto him he hurled the dirt into the face of the left most man, temporarily blinding him.

As the would be killer rubbed his eyes, the centurion dodged the thrust of the other man's spatha, moving deftly to one side. Then, he spun around and slashed at the man's sword arm with his dagger, but did not connect. By now, the second attacker had almost finished removing the dirt from his eyes and the pair were about to regroup. It was at this point that Versillius realised that he was behaving like a complete idiot. His assailants might prefer to attack in silence, but there was no such constraint upon him. As the three men circled each other, with nobody making the first move, he yelled, very loudly, "Night watch, I need the night watch and RIGHT NOW!. Your centurion is under attack."

The two attackers glanced at each other again, but then moved towards him for a further assault. Sidestepping their blows for a third time, he brandished his dagger at them, while shouting even louder, "Come on men, I needy our help. IMMMEDIATLY!...And not tomorrow, please!" After a few seconds, while he carefully avoided further sword thrusts and made several wild slashes at his attackers, a voice from the ramparts of the fort wall yelled, "Is that you calling, centurion...are you in trouble?"

"Of course I am, soldier. Would I be bellowing and waking the whole settlement for any other reason?"

The two attackers suddenly froze and turning away, ran off towards the north, in the direction of the Wall. Aiming his dagger, Versillius hurled it at the man on the right, missing him by a whisker. While he was trying to retrieve the weapon, Marcus and two men of the night guard appeared from out of the southern gate. The centurion explained what had happened and with the younger soldier by his side, returned to the barracks, flanked by the two men of the watch. He had told them that there was no point in chasing his attackers, as they had a head start. Marcus gave the instruction for the watch to be extra vigilant and mount extra patrols along the Wall, before he accompanied the senior officer to his rooms.

"Do you think that it was a revenge attack for our action earlier today, sir?" the junior soldier asked, as he shut the door. Then, turning to his superior officer, he continued, "I certainly detected no activity on the other side of the Wall, this evening."

Versillius, who was shaking more than a little, had to pause and re gather his composure, before he could reply, "I suppose it could be some form of retaliation by the Picts. But I'm not totally convinced. Something out there was not quite right. They may have been wearing torn trousers and their upper bodies were covered in blue paint. And they were both carrying the long sword. But the way that they used it, owed more to Roman training than barbarian warfare. And now that I think about it, my attackers' hair was far too short for them to have been real barbarians."

Marcus then thought for a few moments as he considered Versillius' words. Then, he said, in a measured voice, "As far as I can remember, the men that we killed earlier today were tattooed with blue ink. I don't remember seeing any blue paint on their bodies. Do you suspect that your assailants were Romans or Britons disguised as Picts, centurion?"

"I don't know what to think, at the moment, Marcus. I'd like nothing more that to search the settlement from top to bottom. But as you have only four men to patrol the Wall, that will not happen. Besides, I am in no mood to rouse the whole garrison. Instead, I will go and get some sleep. You should do likewise, as we've both had a long day," Versillius replied.

"But sir, I have my duties as watch commander to perform..."

"Then delegate them, soldier," the centurion countered, "Tell the men that you have my instructions to take an early night. And thank you for appearing so promptly when I was under attack. I realise that you probably saved my life, young man. One pugio against two spathae represents very bad odds."

Marcus smiled and answered, "Don't worry, we'll crack this one yet, sir. After all, the list of suspects is narrowing by the day."

"Although thanks to the legate's instructions we were unable to make any progress today..."

The two men looked at each other, as the same thought occurred to them both, simultaneously. Marcus said, "Perhaps, the general may also have found it convenient, if we had not returned from our military action, earlier today."

When Versillius responded, it was with agitation in his voice. He was angered by the thought that the punishment raid had been nothing but a set up. He said, "I'm not saying that you are wrong, but we need some proof and a good motive. If we make any accusations against the legate and are proved wrong, then I strongly suspect Appius Severus will forget that Constantine abolished crucifixion!"

The younger man than asked about the prefect's feast. Versillius explained about the legate's demeanour, how he had fucked Drusilla in the prefect's vomitarium and his request for sole access to the treasury. He also told him of Gaius Flavius' misgivings about giving the legate unsupervised access to the treasury. Both men considered the senior officer's behaviour, as extremely suspicious. Marcus went onto say, "As you just said, sir, we need some proof, before we dare to repeat these words outside of your quarters."

"We'll see what tomorrow brings," Versillius countered, "I'd be very grateful if you would wake me early in the morning, Marcus. We can bathe together, before I meet with the prefect, and talk about the investigation. There are some very hard and unpleasant decisions that need to be made."

The younger man bowed his head in acknowledgement and was about to leave the centurion's rooms, when Versillius asked, "Marcus, before you go, can you tell me if there were any problems, in either the tavern or brothel tonight? After hearing of the trouble caused by legate's men yesterday, I asked Cominius to station a small detail in the eastern vicus."

"I know of no such trouble, sir, and have been on duty since the sun fell. The settlement was very quiet tonight. Well, that was until you summoned our assistance. In fact, Cominius' patrol returned just before you called for our assistance and told me that they had no trouble to report."

After the younger man had departed, the centurion contemplated the day's final events for a few moments. The legate's bodyguards had obviously not been to the tavern or house of pleasure that night. Perhaps they had been given other duties to attend to by the legate. But feeling exhausted, after everything that had happened in the course of the day, he decided that it was time to sleep. At the side of his bed, he placed a chair, on which he put his unsheathed gladius. He then removed his caligae, bolted the door securely and climbed into the bed, still wearing his tunica and trousers. As he fell asleep, the thought of the legate and Drusilla having it away in the vomitarium was still making him smile. Virgin priestess, my arse, was his last thought before he nodded off.

Chapter Twenty Nine

Marcus was as good as his unspoken word from the previous night. He raised the centurion promptly, as dawn broke. It was far too promptly for the older man's liking, as he was still feeling tired and aching from the previous day's tribulations. He rose from his bed and unlocked the door, after he had sheathed and taken up his sword. Outside the room, Versillius was pleased to see that Marcus was also armed. He put on his caligae and paenula and thanked the young legionnaire for his trouble. They then departed for the communal lavatories, prior to visiting the bathhouses. As they walked through the southern gate, the centurion noted that both the western and eastern forum were deserted. There was not even any sign of the traders setting up their market stalls. It was the fourth day after the weekend, so the market was closed. Later in the morning, there would be no bustling crowds, haggling over the price of meat or vegetables. Both men were aware that the air was thick with a clinging, early morning mist. These conditions were ideal for an assailant to conceal himself. So they walked purposefully, with their hands clasped on their sword handles.

As they reached the first of the public facilities, Versillius said, to the younger man, "I'm sure that one day, the sun will reappear. My ageing bones are finding it very difficult to function properly, in this constant rain, mist and damp."

"It's not much easier for myself, centurion," was his junior's diplomatic reply.

Given the early hour, it was no surprise to find that inside the toilets there was only one other person present. Their fellow early riser was Artemis, the

Physician. He greeted them perfunctorily and without any warmth, as they lowered their trousers and sat on the seats opposite him. To the centurion's great relief, the red wine and olive oil had done its work. For the first time in several months, his turds plopped out without any effort. While he was cleaning himself with the leaves, he couldn't help noticing that both the physician and Marcus were struggling. Stifling a smile, he said to Artemis, "I'm glad to see you here today, doctor. If we hadn't been sent north, across the border yesterday, then I would have come to your surgery. The second murder, of Partimius, has put you in the clear. As you had no disagreements with him, professionally or financially, I have officially removed you from our enquiries."

The physician raised his eyebrows, and replied, with a grimace on his red face, "Damn this constipation! It's all very well you offering me a half apology, centurion, but I will not forget this. Maybe you were doing your job, but for a man like me to be accused of..." He suddenly fell silent and a big smile rippled across his face, as a large, firm stool eventually dropped from his anus. Artemis sighed, before resuming, "But I still stand by my words about Antonius. He was a snivelling, little clerk and nothing more. Although, I am very sorry that Partimius was murdered. He was by far the better and more reasonable man to deal with."

At the centurion's side Marcus groaned with pleasure, as he finally forced his turds out. But their joint feeling of well being was short lived, because Septimus a young and junior official in the administration, entered the lavatories and said to the two soldiers, "Thank the deities that I have found you, centurion. The prefect has not yet arrived at the civic buildings. Yesterday, he made specific arrangements to meet with me, early in the morning. We have urgent business to attend to, concerning the legate's audit. It is due to take place in less than two hours. But there is no sign of the prefect anywhere!"

"Calm down, man," Versillius replied, to the slightly built and unusually blond haired youth, "Gaius Flavius had a late night entertaining the legate and the governor. He also arranged for me to meet with him, to assist in the inspection, after bathing. Did you try the baths?"

"Of course, that was the first place where I looked. He's not there..." Septimus answered, as his voice tailed off.

Have you been to his villa? Perhaps he may have overslept," Versillius responded, unsure as to reason behind the young clerk's fevered demeanour.

"What, me, go to his villa?" the young man replied, "I wouldn't dare do that. There's no way that I have sufficient seniority to disturb him at his home. That's why I decided to look for you and Marcus in the barracks. The day time watch told me that you would be either in here or in the baths."

Versillius realised that his hopes of having a long soak in the warm pool were now dashed. As Marcus carefully wiped his bottom, the centurion said, "Septimus, return to your office. I'll go and wake the prefect for you. We both had a lot of red wine to drink last night. If I had not been roused by Marcus, then I dare say, that I would still be in my bed, fast asleep."

The young clerk bowed respectfully to the centurion and left the latrines. The two military men then raised their trousers and left Artemis to continue with his labours. This was a pity, because after their conversation the previous day, Versillius had thought of a question for the Greek physician. After the doctor's earlier accusation that the Romans had stolen all their culture and medicine from the Greeks, the centurion wanted to ask him how much his own people had "borrowed" from the Egyptians.

Chapter Thirty

The two men crossed the via south and soon reached the western vicus, where the mist was thicker and showed no sign of lifting. As they approached the prefect's villa, the centurion scanned the building anxiously. He could not hear any noises coming from the inside of the building. A quick glance at the roof showed no sign of any smoke rising from the main chimney. After knocking on the front door several times and getting no response, he tried to open it, but the main entrance was securely barred. The centurion than asked Marcus to bang heavily on the door, as his own hands were starting to feel quite sore. But the younger man's pounding still produced no answer from inside. Beginning to feel worried, he started to circle the building, looking for any signs of a forced entry. At the back of the villa his fears were realised, when he found a small side window, which had been put through. Summoning the slimmer and junior soldier, he said, "You'd better climb in, as your limbs are younger and more supple than mine. Unbolt the rear door, so that we can see what's happened in there."

Marcus carefully eased himself into the villa, through the side window, and within a minute had opened the back door. He said, "It was already unlocked and unbolted, sir...this isn't very good, is it?"

Versillius entered the building and swiftly moved towards the sleeping area, shouting, "Prefect, are you awake? You're late for your meeting with Septimus, at the civic offices..."

Receiving no reply, Versillius drew his sword and started to feel even more concerned for the prefect's and Juliana's safety. But while they walked through the kitchen area, he realised immediately that Gaius

Flavius was unlikely to be awake. The old slave, who normally answered the door to the prefect's visitors, was lying face up on the floor. There was a pool of congealed blood around the body's left hand side. And the remains of his broken clay lamp were littered around the kitchen floor.

Although the early morning light was not very good, due to the mist, the centurion was able to see that the slave had been stabbed in the heart. But unlike the earlier murders, the wound did not appear to have been caused by a narrow sword. Versillius touched the dead man's face and felt that the flesh was cold, meaning that he had been dead for some time. Unable to do anything to help the unfortunate slave, they then continued to move cautiously towards the villa's sleeping quarters, all the time expecting the worst. The slave had most certainly been killed in the night. If the slave's body still lay undiscovered by the prefect, at this time of the morning, then the chances were that he and his wife had met a similar fate. Marcus and Versillius entered the master bedroom, to discover a scene of absolute carnage.

Gaius Flavius and Juliana had been butchered, presumably as they had slept in their bed. The centurion was aghast, as he looked at the blood stained bodies lying on the soiled bedclothes. The prefect was slumped on top of Juliana, as if he had been trying to protect her, before he died. Both men saw the sword cuts on his hands, which showed that he had tried to grab their attackers' weapons, as the fatal blows had rained down on him. Their mortal wounds were caused by deep slashes to the body and the neck. But the centurion told himself that a gladius could slash, as well as stab, especially if the victims were lying down in a bed. Although he knew inside himself that was not the case. Like the slave's murderer, the prefect's killers had been wielding the spatha. Turning to Marcus, he said, "I feel that this is all my fault. If only I'd raised the garrison after you had rescued me last night. Perhaps, I am getting too old for this job..."

"You're being too hard on yourself, sir," the younger legionnaire replied, "There was no way that any of us could foresee this happening. Besides, the intruders ran northwards, towards the wall."

"Yes, but then they must have doubled back and then done this..."

While the centurion was speaking, Marcus closely examined the two bodies on the bed. After a few moments he grasped the bedclothes and said, "This is very interesting, sir. If you look closely, there are distinct traces of a blue colour on the white sheets. Can you see it, centurion?"

Versillius looked at the linen and saw that alongside the bloodstains, it was coloured by a blue stain. From there, it was a short leap to remember his attackers from the previous night. It confirmed his view that Gaius Flavius had died because of his negligence. As the older man bit his lip, Marcus started to shake his head, from side to side. "You think this is the work of the Picts, don't you, sir? Well, I certainly do not!" Marcus stated, "Remember, what I said to you in your quarters, last night. They have blue tattoos on their bodies and do not wear blue war paint. And unless I am badly mistaken, the legate's bodyguard carry the long swords."

"But the first two murders were caused by a gladius. Now, we have the spatha to contend with. Whatever happened here, there is more than one murderer at large in Virulanium." Versillius desperately wanted the young man to be right. But even if he was correct, it was not going to help the prefect or his wife. The centurion tried to put aside his feelings of guilt and continued, "So we may have soldiers in this settlement, pretending to be Picts. All we have to do now is prove it..." He then walked over to Juliana and stroked her cheek gently saying, "Forgive me and sleep well, gracious lady. I hope that you have a safe journey to the under world. Your son will already be there, waiting to welcome you. I'll ensure that both yourself and Gaius Flavius have the proper rites, to help you on your way." Then looking at the body of the prefect, Versillius said, "You tried very hard to pretend to be a miserable, old cunt with a bad temper. But do not think that you fooled me for one moment. Travel swiftly to your eternal repose, friend..."

"Where are their other servants, sir?" Marcus asked, as the centurion finished making his farewells, puzzled by their absence.

"The hour is still early and the night of the feast was late. I suspect that the prefect told them to come in later than usual. They're probably still asleep in the safety of their thatched houses."

Returning to the kitchen, Versillius removed a set of keys from the dead slave's belt and unlocked the front door. As he stood at the front of the villa, taking in the air and wondering what to do next, a party of four fully armoured soldiers entered the grounds. The centurion immediately recognised Lucian Flavius, the leader of the legate's bodyguard. Nepius Pertinax, the tall, bearded legionnaire and two other men accompanied him. All four carried long swords, suspended from their baldric belts. They seemed surprised to find the centurion standing outside the prefect's front door. Lucian halted the detail and said to him, "I thought that this was the prefect's villa, rather than yours. He's late for his meeting with the legate. We're here to find out what's going on."

Versillius thought carefully for a moment, before replying, "It is an appointment that he will never be able to keep. Gaius Flavius and his wife were slaughtered in their beds last night. Obviously, sometime after the feast, given in the legate's honour, had finished. Whoever did it was wearing blue body paint..."

Pertinax smirked and stated loudly, "Well, centurion, I think that might be down to you. If you prefer to mount a guard around the tavern and brothel, rather than protecting your civic officials, then I'd say that it is just as well that you are about to retire!"

Versillius looked up at him and replied, angrily, "No soldier in the Roman army has the right to address a centurion in that manner, whatever legate they report to. When I return to the barracks you will be physically punished for those comments. This time, you will not be allowed the luxury of facing me on the training ground. I shall personally ensure that you feel the rods of my men."

The other two soldiers, Vitellius and Decius, stiffened and bristled at centurion's words. Pertinax, seemingly unperturbed, answered, "I don't think old man. It's more likely to be you who will be feeling the rods, after what has happened here..."

"That will not happen in my fort, you useless, lanky streak of bearded piss!" Versillius yelled, starting to lose his temper. Marcus suddenly moved towards him, not wanting his superior officer to do anything stupid. The hirsute soldier was also angry and reached for his sword, but Lucian placed his hand on the man's arm, before saying, "I think we should all go and inform the legate about this. Now that he has audited the temple, he is anxious to finish his work in the civic buildings. Then we can return to Deva and leave the soldiers of Virulanium to sort out their problems with the northern neighbours. That is, if they are capable of doing so..."

Chapter Thirty One

When they reached the barracks, Versillius and Marcus were kept waiting outside the centurion's office. Lucian went inside and briefed the legate on the events that had happened at the prefect's villa. While they were sitting there, Pertinax maintained the constant irritating, smile on his bruised features, as he stared directly at Versillius. The centurion had to admire the cheek of the man. Nobody could have deduced from his attitude and insults, that Versillius had emerged victorious from their confrontation on the training ground. To make matters worse, the bearded legionnaire seemed to have also recently developed a further annoying habit. Every few seconds he nodded his head, in the general direction of the centurion's office. This was done in conjunction with a raising of his eyebrows. Both Versillius and Marcus found that their right hands kept wandering down towards their sword handles. But the centurion reminded himself that now was not the time to settle scores. He promised himself that the final reckoning would come soon and he would certainly relish it. Versillius was sure that he would enjoy the moment far more than he had enjoyed smacking Pertinax in his testicles, the previous day. And he had really relished delivering that stunning blow.

The group of legionnaires were not alone outside the centurion's office. Aulus Falerius and his colleague from Eboracum, Tertius Plinius, were also waiting on the legate. Versillius nodded to the two merchants, who both seemed quite anxious. They could see and feel the tension between the legate's soldiers and the two men from the garrison. Aulus Falerius said to him, "Personally, I've got no idea what is happening in this vicus. But we just want permission from Appius Severus to return to Eboracum. We've travelled all the way from Deva with him and there doesn't seem to be even the slightest prospect of us making even a single sale! It's time to cut our losses and return home."

"Before something happens to us," his colleague, echoed, rather glumly.

The centurion has no chance to respond to the merchants because Lucian emerged from his office and ushered the two legionnaires from Virulanium in. As they had both expected, the legate had a severe expression on his patrician face. Turning to the two soldiers he said to them, " Versillius, you've now managed to lose the prefect and his wife to the marauding Picts. I told you yesterday evening, that you should have slaughtered their whole village. But you did not. Just look at what has happened in this settlement in recent days..."

"From what perspective am I supposed to be looking at these events, Appius Severus?" the centurion retorted, halting the commanding officer in full flow.

The legate was less than pleased to be interrupted and continued, "You will listen to me in silence, soldier. It's bad enough losing two scribes to the barbarians. But you have let the administration's most senior civic official be killed as well. That strikes me as rank incompetence on your part. And that's not to mention the personal inconvenience that I have suffered. Do you realise that I spent almost an hour inside your dreary principae waiting for the prefect to appear?"

Marcus swallowed and replied, on his superiors behalf, "Legate, there is absolutely no evidence that the Picts are responsible for any of the murders. I maintained the watch last night and I can assure you that there were no incursions from the north, across the Wall."

The legate totally ignored Marcus and glanced up at Versillius before saying, "I understand from your man, Trajanius, that you were attacked on by two tribesmen, after leaving the prefect's villa. Or, were you not planning to tell me about that incident, Versillius?"

"They may have been Picts, but they could also have been our men wearing blue body paint," he responded, "And for good measure, when they tried to kill me they were wielding the same swords that your men carry."

"This will not do," the legate retorted, with a great deal of exasperation in his voice, "When will you stop harping on about swords? I have already told you that the barbarians could have stolen our weapons at any time, over the past two hundred years. What I want to know, is why didn't you despatch the watch in pursuit of your attackers, after you had been rescued?"

"Because they had headed north with a good start. Bear in mind, that most of the soldiers on duty last night had been across the border, yesterday. I had no desire to raise a tired garrison that had previously been acting on your specific instructions."

Appius Severus stood up and strolled around the desk, his hands clasped behind his back. After a short time he smiled and said, "I did not care for or like your implications about the swords that my bodyguards carry. But I can see why you are trying to take others down with you. This is undoubtedly a fine mess. I suppose that as the legate and commanding officer, I must take some form of action and you two must take the blame. Versillius, I am sorry to end your military career in such a fashion, but due to your repeated dereliction of duty, I am bringing your retirement forward by two months. You can, and will, return to civilian life with immediate effect. Of course, this means that you will get no pension, as you have not yet completed your twenty-five years of service. But under Roman military law, you do of course have the right to appeal to the governor, against my decision,"

"What sort of justice is this?" the centurion retorted, "The governor would not know if he needed a piss or a shit in the morning, without your express directions!"

"Exactly," Appius Severus replied, smiling at the former centurion, "I think that you are beginning to get my drift, Versillius. Now, Marcus Pontius, I have also considered your position and actions in this sorry set of events. I have decided to reduce you to the ranks, and remove you from the post of night watch commander. And the two of you can thank your lucky stars that I am in a good mood today. Otherwise, I would be minded to order some kind of physical punishment."

"But that leaves Virulanium without a prefect, centurion or a night watch commander," Versillius said. He did not know whether to feel more distressed for himself or Marcus. The younger man's face was completely crestfallen.

"I had thought about that, before I spoke, believe it or not. As the legion's commanding officer it is also a part of my job to consider the alternative. My man Lucian Flavius will act as the settlement's centurion. That is, until a full time replacement is appointed. He will also take over the conduct of the murder investigation from which you are both removed. Especially you Versillius, as you are no longer a serving officer. Under Lucian's command, I have no doubt that the Picts will finally learn the lesson that you failed to teach them."

The legate then turned to Marcus and stared at him, before going onto say, "As for the night watch, I will ask the legionnaire Trajanius to take over that responsibility. He seems like a competent enough fellow to me. Now gentlemen, you must excuse me. With or without the late prefect, I have an important audit and census to conclude at the civic buildings. You are both dismissed from my presence."

The two men walked out of the former centurion's office. Marcus in particular looked visibly distressed, feeling that his career was now in ruins. Versillius was more contemplative, silently considering an ignominious end to what was almost twenty-five years of military service. The prospect of retirement without a pension was particularly annoying. During the entire term of his service, regular deductions had been taken from his salary. These were enforced by the administration, so that a soldier would not be able to retire without a nest egg. Now the legate had taken that away from him, dispensing justice that could only be described as summary, at best. In such circumstances, the last thing that either of them needed was to see were the asinine, grinning features of Pertinax, as they emerged into the corridor. The tall legionnaire opened his mouth, as if to speak. But seeing the stern expressions on both men's faces, as they looked at him directly, he thought better of it. Versillius decided not to think better of it and said to the man, "There will be a settling of scores, soldier, and I for one am anticipating it with great relish!"

Pertinax did not reply. In all likelihood, he was remembering the beating that he had taken from the centurion, on the previous day. Behind the tall soldier, the two merchants from Eboracum grimaced and begged Lucian Flavius to hasten their audience with the legate.

Chapter Thirty Two

As they left the barracks building and emerged into a light shower, Marcus turned to Versillius and said, "I know that it's early in the day, but could you persuade Caracalla to open up his tavern for us? For once, I most certainly need a beer or two. The loss of your pension is undoubtedly a serious blow, for which I am extremely sorry, sir. But from my own selfish perspective, the prospect of reporting to Lucian and Trajanius is more than enough to drive me to drink!"

Now that he was out of Pertinax's direct proximity, the centurion's usual equanimity had returned. He grinned at the younger man's words and answered, "I'm sure that you must have realised by now, that it's never to early for me to visit the tavern. But first, I think we should make the arrangements for the funerals of Gaius Flavius and his wife. I'll sort out the building of the pyres, if you arrange a detail to transport the bodies, once Lucian releases them from the crime scene. Then we can meet in the bar and sink those beers."

Marcus returned to the barracks, and Versillius left the fort and crossed the empty forum. Ignoring the rain, he walked through the eastern vicus and headed towards the traders' thatched houses. There he commissioned the building of three pyres, from the same local craftsman that Partimius had dealt with. The former centurion wanted the old slave to get the same passage to the underworld as his master. He knew that the prefect would have wanted his old retainer to be taken care of. After paying the trader in advance, the centurion retraced his steps back to the fort. On the way there, he met up with Marcus, who was standing just outside the southern gate. The younger soldier assured him that despite his own demotion, he had experienced no problems in finding volunteers for the detail – once Lucian was able to release the bodies. By the time they reached the tavern, Caracalla had just opened for business and was surprised to see the two legionnaires approach his premises. This was because the sun had only recently reached its mid point. The two men entered his bar and sat down at the centurion's usual table. Versillius called for two large beers. As the bar owner placed the clay tankards in front of them, he said, "Let me thank you for stationing that detail of legionnaires, in the vicus last night. To my great relief, there was no trouble here, whatsoever. In fact, I didn't even see the strangers from Deva. I suspect that they must have known that you were taking special precautions. Now, this is getting to be a bad habit on my part, but please, have this one on me."

They thanked the bar owner, who seeing that the two men wanted to talk privately, returned to his duties. Marcus looked anxiously at the centurion and said, "Where do we go now? Are you going to appeal to the governor?"

Versillius stroked his chin and replied, "This is by no means over. Although, I have no confidence in appealing to the governor, while the legate is still around. But I'm sure that there is a way out. If we crack the murders, then I'll get my pension back and your seniority will be restored."

"But how can we do that? The legate ordered us to stop our investigations with immediate effect."

"We still have our brains, limbs and swords," the centurion answered, "And hopefully the capability to still use the three of them. If you do not want to continue the enquiry, then I will understand it. After all, you are still an enlisted man. But as I have been dismissed from the service, then I am under no such compunction."

The young man drained his beaker, and before calling Caracalla to bring two more beers said, "I'll help you as much as I can, Versillius. From my very first day in the imperial army, which was over five years ago, you have always treated me decently. Just tell me what you want and when you need it."

He fell silent, as the bar owner refilled their beakers from his heavy, clay jug. When he had departed, Versillius replied, "I thank you for your offer of assistance. But let me just bounce a few ideas off you for the moment. We have two dead scribes, along with the prefect and his wife, not to mention the slave. An attempt was made on my life last night. I have no doubt that the legate, rather than the governor is behind all of this, but I can't for the life of me understand what his motive is!"

"Why do you discount the governor so easily?" Marcus responded.

"Like I told Appius Severus, in my former office, the man does not know his own mind. He's incapable of organising a round of drinks in this bar, let alone five murders and one attempted killing. I'm convinced that the legate is our man. Let us remember, that apart from Antonius, the deaths started on the very day that he arrived in Virulanium."

Marcus considered his words carefully, before saying, "And the chief scribe was murdered the night before he came here. But the legate could not have carried out the murders himself. The man doesn't even carry a weapon..."

"Use your brains, soldier," the centurion replied, "He brought four bodyguards with him from Deva, including that grinning idiot, Pertinax. When you return to the fort take great care not to show him your back."

"Or Trajanius, as well for that matter," Marcus responded, glumly, "After the discipline that I have imposed on him, since I took command of the night watch. I'm quite sure that right now, he's sat down in the barracks, rubbing his hands, in anticipation of returning the favours."

Versillius nodded at him and said, "Taking command is never an easy task, as I know well, to my own cost. But you may have hit upon something useful there. Now, I realise that I am always talking about sword wounds, as Appius Severus kindly pointed out. But we must not forget that the first two murders were caused by the gladius. For some reason, the legate has a high opinion of Trajanius. Maybe these two facts are connected."

Marcus pondered the thrust of his argument and said, "Trajanius and the legate. That's a very interesting angle. Since the death of the prefect, we have forgotten about the miscreant legionnaire and his little cult. I'll see what I can find out in the barracks, when I have finished in here. But what about the proconsul in Eboracum? He might not be in Virulanium, but if he is involved in the revival of Mithras that would rule the legate out."

Versillius rose from his seat and said, "Unfortunately, I must leave you to your beer now. I need to speak to Flavala, and let her know what has happened this morning. I'll be next door, should you need me."

As he departed, Marcus called across the bar, for Caracalla to bring him another drink. On his way out, the former centurion thought that this had to be a first. Not only was the younger man staying in the tavern longer than himself, but he was also going to drink at least one more beer than he had consumed.

Chapter Thirty Three

The brothel owner answered his calls from the street and admitted the former soldier into the house of pleasure. Flavala looked at his black eye, the legacy of his fight with Pertinax. It almost matched the bruise that the bearded legionnaire had given her, two nights earlier. But as they walked through the frescoed corridor, to her private apartments, she could see from his demeanour that there was something seriously wrong. Concerned for his well being, she said to him, "Tell me, why you are looking so sad, Versillius? What has happened?"

He swallowed heavily, and replied, "Flavala, I'm very sorry. But I am here to formally withdraw my proposal of marriage to you. The legate has dismissed me from the army, this very morning, two months short of my pension. Despite my strong feelings and longing for a life with you, I now have no prospect of any future income. So I am unable to support a wife and home."

Her unpinned auburn hair glinted in the mid day sun, which had briefly appeared from behind the clouds. The light was shining through an open window and silhouetted her shapely figure. Without any hesitation, she answered, "I'll be the judge of when you can withdraw your proposal and what you can and cannot support. But first, explain to me in detail what has taken place. I've already been told about your exploits on the training ground, with Pertinax. And that was something that I told you to leave well alone!"

Versillius told her about his dinner with the prefect and the legate's overbearing attitude and his liaison with Drusilla. He described his subsequent escape from death, on the way back to the barracks. He went on to relate the events that had occurred on the following morning, starting with the discoveries at the prefect's villa. He ending with the dressing down that he and Marcus had received from Appius Severus. When he had finished speaking, Flavala thought briefly before replying, "Poor Juliana, I shall miss our chats in the market place. Honestly, Versillius, I do not know what is happening in this vicus at the moment. But about yourself, my husband to be...under Roman law you are unable to withdraw your proposal, without my assent. If you do, I can sue you for breach of promise."

"Sue me for what? I barely have a denarius left to my name. All my savings went into the villa, on the eastern side of the vicus."

She had a very mischievous smile on her face, as she said to him, "But I have more than enough money to engage a lawyer or a scribe, were there one to be had in Virulanium these days."

"Even if you send for a lawyer from Banna, it will do you no good. I tell you that I am penniless, woman."

Flavala looked offended at his words and said, "You can be very stupid at times, Versillius. I have no intention whatsoever to sue you for breach of promise. It was just my little joke, but I can see that you are in no mood for humour."

"I'm sorry, but being dismissed from the army two months before completing my twenty five years, has left my laughing glands slightly depleted..."

Flavala moved across the room and wrapped her arms around Versillius, telling him as she pressed her body against his, "Don't be a fool, Versillius. You have no reason to withdraw your proposal. I have more than enough money to keep the both of us. And do you want to know something else, a secret which I have kept for a long time?"

"What?" he asked, as his body responded to her touch. The centurion's hands touched her breasts and then gently caressed her firm buttocks, as he awaited her reply.

"When you were a younger man, I hated to take money from you after we had sex. I wanted to give you myself for free and that feeling has never left me. Now, I don't want to hear another word from you. There are twelve rooms in this house, take me to the one that has the speciality that you desire. Then, we can turn the time back twenty five years, to when you were a raw recruit...in more than one way!"

They kissed deeply and he took her to the room with the fresco that depicted a woman kneeling in front of a man, offering herself to him. They entered the chamber and fell together onto the padded stone couch. He had already removed his sword, but as she started to undo his trousers and fondle his erect penis, they heard Marcus calling from the street, yelling, "Centurion, you must come quickly. There has been yet another murder."

His cock deflated instantly and Flavala uttered a loud groan of frustration. As he secured his trousers, she said, "I want to see you back here later, Versillius, as you have unfinished business to attend to. And tomorrow, whether you like it or not, I am going to start making arrangements for our wedding. So I do not want to hear any more nonsense about you withdrawing your offer of marriage. But I wouldn't mind hearing you tell me that you love me. That is, if you really do..."

"I do love you, Flavala, more than you can ever know. And I promise to prove it to your satisfaction tonight. That is a vow which will not be broken."

She nodded as he replaced his gladius, saying to him, "Just be careful with yourself, out there soldier. I want you you and that big cock back in one piece..."

Then after ensuring that his trousers were not about to fall down, Versillius emerged from the house of pleasure, into the daylight.

Chapter Thirty Four

Outside the brothel, Marcus having noted the centurion's flushed features, said, "Sir, I do hope that I wasn't interrupting anything between yourself and Flavala. But as I was sat in the bar, Quintillus the acolyte to Drusilla, entered. He had been wandering around the forum, in a very agitated state. When he saw me he told me straight away that the priestess was dead! He found her murdered in the temple. Then he insisted that I go and find you."

Versillius glanced up at the now cloudy sky, as if he was seeking inspiration from above, and replied, "So he didn't know that we had been removed from the case. News has not travelled as fast as it normally does in the settlement."

"I asked him to wait for us outside the temple, thinking that you would want to question him. That is, if you still intend to continue with the investigation."

"Of course I do and we will go to see Quintillus immediately. Listen Marcus, I'm happy for you to accompany me, but you are taking a very grave chance. As a private citizen, I can proceed with the investigation, but if you are discovered at the latest crime scene there could be serious repercussions for you."

The younger soldier grinned, before answering, "The legate can go and screw himself. As you said earlier, we still have our brains, limbs and weapons. Hopefully, we can put them to some good use and sort this business out once and for all."

"My feelings exactly", Versillius retorted, as the two men quickened their pace. He had not expressed any false remorse about the death of Drusilla. To do so would have been hypocritical on his part. Her murder affected his feelings in no particular way, other than a hope that this would be the last of the killings. Passing the tavern and the southern gate, the two men walked into the western forum and approached the temple. By this time, the mist had lifted from the empty forum, but the atmosphere was still quite eerie and very quiet. They found Quintillus sitting on the stone steps that lead up to the portico. He was a lean man, in his early twenties and his long tunica and toga were bleached white. As the temple's acolyte, he had been Drusilla's assistant for several years. When he saw the two soldiers, he rose to his feet and said, "It's terrible, centurion, our priestess has been murdered..."

"When did you find her body, Quintillus?" Versillius asked.

"Less than thirty minutes ago. Drusilla had given me the morning off, as she had to attend to the census and audit with the legate. The priestess told me that I would only get in the way and that I was to report back to work after the sun had reached its zenith."

The centurion raised his eyebrows and after climbing the stone steps, led the two other men into the temple. As his eyes adjusted to the relative darkness inside, the acolyte struck a flint and lit a torch. He then took them to the votive altar, where Versillius saw the body of the priestess slumped on the floor. Taking the torch from Quintillus he examined the corpse. To his surprise he found the tell tale, narrow wounds of the gladius, in her stomach. Marcus crouched down and said, "It's the same type of weapon that was used on the scribes, centurion. We have to put a stop to this, before any more of our citizens are murdered."

"Oh, but there's more for you to see, soldiers," Quintillus cut in, "The temple's strong room has been raided. If you look over there, you will see that the door is ajar."

They walked over to the thick iron door, which was open. The small room behind it, which housed the temple's assets, was empty. It should have been filled with hundreds of votive offerings and thousands of coins. The acolyte said, "I don't like to accuse anybody, but the fact that this has happened on the very day that the audit was carried out, makes me suspicious. The priestess was always most reluctant to unlock this room, unless she was depositing a valuable offering inside it. And she most certainly would never have left it unlocked, while she still had breath in her body."

The exact same thought had already occurred to both Marcus and the centurion. They were also aware of the legate's next port of call, the town's treasury. Turning to Quintillus the former soldier said, "Tell nobody else about this and lock the temple doors. I want you to remain here, because it is important that the news travels no further. That will give us the time that we need to put an end to this evil."

The acolyte inclined his head and promised to follow the centurion's instructions but asked, nervously, "Are you sure that I'll be safe, centurion?"

"Now that your temple had been robbed, you are probably in the safest place in Virulanium. However, where we are going is likely to be rather different..." was Versillius' terse reply.

Chapter Thirty Five

The two men crossed the western forum swiftly. As they walked together, back towards the southern gate, Marcus asked, "Have you figured it out yet, centurion?"

"I think so and it's all to do with money. Our civic funds and the assets of the temple. You must remember that we are the wealthiest settlement in the area. But we are also the least well defended in number of soldiers. What better place to stage a robbery? Especially on the market's rest day, when the forum is empty?" Versillius replied. They re-entered the fort by the southern gate and approached the principae. At the main entrance to the civic buildings, they drew their swords, as a precaution. Then Versillius led Marcus into the building where the treasury was sited. After the recent spate of deaths, neither man was surprised to find the offices empty and quiet. Moving in silence, through the long corridors, they walked towards the treasury. To their dismay, they found the body of Septimus in a side office, his throat slit. With great resolve in his voice, Versillius whispered, "I hope that we are not too late. This ends now - and it must end here!"

The treasury was sited towards the rear of the civic offices, on the western side of the fort's walls. Within a few moments they had reached it, to find the entrance locked. Like the entrance to the temple's treasury, the doors were made of strong metal. The centurion raised a finger to his lips and they both listened intently. There were sounds of movement coming from the inside of the fortified room. "What can we do now?" Marcus whispered.

Versillius smiled and removed from his belt the ring of master keys, which he had not surrendered to the legate. Very gently, he inserted the key for the treasury into the door's lock and turned it slowly. Then he patiently eased the door open. The two men entered the strong room, their weapons still unsheathed. Once inside, they saw the four legionnaires of the legate's bodyguard; Lucian Flavius, Vitellius, Decius and Nepius Pertinax. They were standing outside the treasury's side door, which was open and unbolted. This was an emergency exit, which backed onto unused land, adjacent to the fort's western wall. In front of the side exit was a horse drawn cart. The legate's four soldiers were busily loading it up with sacks, filled with the coins and bullion of the civic treasury. The two men moved silently forwards, towards the legate's bodyguard. In the cart, the centurion could not only see the spoils from Virulanium's treasury, but also the missing votive offerings from the temple.

"That will do gentlemen. Your game is over now!" he said, when they were within six feet of the side exit. His words took the four soldiers by surprise. Lucian Fulvius was the first to react, but he didn't get a chance to draw his spatha. Marcus launched himself at the legionnaire and in one thrusting, stabbing movement impaled him on his gladius. Meanwhile, Versillius had taken similar action against Decius, the soldier closest to him, dealing a slashing blow to his face. As the two men crumpled to the ground, their remaining colleagues finally drew their own swords and advanced towards them.

"I'll take Pertinax," Versillius shouted, "As this is for real, the pleasure will be all mine!"

Marcus to was left to deal with Vitellius. A threat that he was more than capable of dealing with. As he circled his own adversary, Pertinax's demeanour amazed the former centurion. Even under the threat of death in mortal combat, the tall soldier could not remove the inane, stupid grin from his bearded face. The centurion let the man come onto him and easily dodged several spatha thrusts. It was clear, from the standard of his swordsmanship, that the man had never been into battle. All his blows were sloppy and not at all well aimed. Pertinax had also not learnt about the value of counter punching, from their confrontation on the training ground. So after avoiding a few more careless thrusts, Versillius decided that it was time to take the initiative. First, he let the legionnaire lunge at him again. He then executed a sidestep, which totally confused the taller and clumsier man, before thrusting forwards with his own sword. Unable to parry the blow, Pertinax squealed as the cold metal pierced his maile shirt. It cut into his soft flesh, just below the left hand side of his ribs. Thinking of the perfect and Juliana, the centurion twisted the blade, before withdrawing it from the man's side. His opponent collapsed to the ground at the side of the cart. Versillius found it interesting to see that the sides of his lips curled downwards, rather than up, in death.

Looking round he saw that Marcus' adversary had dropped his sword to the ground and was knelt before him begging for mercy. The weight of the stronger and younger legionnaire's blows had soon convinced him of the futility of his cause. Vitellius he had been unable to make any headway against the more seasoned soldier. His sword arm lacked the strength to fend off his opponent for any longer, so he had given up the fight. Marcus seemed unsure as to whether to spare or despatch the man. But before Versillius could tell him to stay his hand, Vitellius shouted, "If you spare me then I'll tell you what you need to know. Just don't kill me, please…"

The tone of desperation in his voice was evident to both soldiers. "We'll take your offer," Versillius replied, hurriedly signalling for Marcus to stay his gladius. As the younger man sheathed his weapon, Vitellius started to talk. Still on his knees, the soldier explained how he and the other men had been acting on the legate's instructions. After he had finished, Marcus gestured for him to rise and bound his prisoner's hands. They then carried the wealth from the civic buildings and the temple back into the treasury. After making sure that the rear door was securely bolted and locked, they did the same for the main entrance. Satisfied that the room was now safe, they led their captive through the silent corridors, towards the main entrance. "I think that we need to talk to the legate," Marcus said, to the centurion, as the three men left the building.

"You are not wrong. But we also need to speak to the governor, as well. Somebody has to pass judgement on this sorry state of affairs. We can only hope that for once, Quintus Lucius will be his own man." he replied.

Their prisoner then said, "You'll find the governor at the barracks with Appius Severus. The legate wanted him away from the civic buildings while we carried out our work. So he deliberately detained him at the barracks, discussing the scope of the audit. I think they'll both be in your office."

"Well, we'd better make our way there. The sooner we confront the legate, then the quicker that this will be finished with, Marcus," Versillius stated. The three men then left the civic buildings, and crossed the parade ground. Two paces in front of Versillius and Marcus, Vitellius walked slowly, with his head bowed. Despite his life being spared for the moment, the man knew that under Roman military law, he faced a most uncertain future. But Versillius suddenly interrupted his thoughts. The centurion had scanned the fort's walls and noticed that there was not another legionnaire in sight.

So he asked Vitellius, "Where is everybody? This fort seems to be as empty as a drunken soldier's purse!"

"You are everybody, sir" the prisoner replied, apprehensively, "The legate sent your century westwards, to check for breaches in the wall. It was to give us a chance to clean out the treasury. I think that he may have held Trajanius back..."

Chapter Thirty Six

When they reached the barracks, the centurion drew his sword. He directed Vitellius towards his former office, which the legate was using as if it were his own. Without bothering to knock, he opened the door and thrust the prisoner into the body of the room. Appius Severus was sat behind his desk, with the governor seated in front of him. Trajanius was stood behind the legate, who was jabbing his finger at the governor. All three men looked shocked to see the bound legionnaire and his two captors. The legate reacted first saying, quite calmly, "You are in serious trouble, Versillius, entering this room with an unsheathed weapon. I was just explaining to the governor about how I had been forced to bring your retirement forward. And now it looks as if you have unlawfully imprisoned one of my men, while he was in the course of carrying out official duties!" Then looking directly at the governor, he stated, "This will just not do, Quintus Lucius, it is an offence punishable by death to interfere with my legitimate orders. Let alone, to threaten our lives with a gladius!" But although his tone was relaxed and imperious, there was just the slightest hint of a tremor in the timbre of his voice.

The white haired governor scratched his head and said, "Perhaps, we'd better have an explanation from the former centurion. Call me old fashioned, but I do so like to hear both sides of a story. Please humour me, Appius Severus, so that we can then put this matter to rest."

"Where are your comrades, Vitellius?" the legate continued, brushing aside the governor's words.

"They are dead, sir. The two legionnaires surprised us in the treasury..."

"Say no more, man. I think that is proof enough, to convince the governor of their guilt," Appius Severus responded, rising to his feet, as if he wanted to leave the office in a hurry. But he noted Marcus stood directly in front of the room's only exit. His hand was by his sword handle. Versillius stood slightly in front of him, clenching his unsheathed gladius. The legate promptly shrugged and sat down again.

"Can somebody please tell me, what exactly is going on here?" Quintus Lucius asked, "I have to say that I find this is all very confusing. Versillius, please sheath your sword. You know that such sharp objects make me feel very nervous."

"There's nothing to be said," was the legate's response, "These two men have killed three members of my personal guard and imprisoned another, while they were fulfilling their official instructions. Trajanius, I order you to summon the daytime watch and have these men arrested and executed."

Versillius grinned and said to Appius Severus, "Trajanius may summon the daytime watch for all that he is worth. But as you despatched them westwards, they will take some time to get here."

"He's right, legate," Trajanius replied, "I did as you told me to do and despatched the garrison to the west. What are we going to do now, pater?"

"You can start by not calling me pater, you infernal idiot," Appius Severus hissed back at him.

The governor started to look even more confused at their exchange and said to Versillius, "I didn't realise that the legate was this man's father. Did you know this? And please put that sword away. I can't feel relaxed until you do..."

The centurion glanced up at Trajanius and said, "Once the heliodromus has thrown over his gladius, I shall sheath mine and explain everything!"

"Do as he says, man!" the governor ordered, still unsure as to the familial relationship between Trajanius and Appius Severus. Trajanius opened his mouth to say something to the legate. Who shook his head, before the legionnaire could speak and indicated for him to follow Versillius' instructions. With a look of resignation on his face, Trajanius removed his baldric belt and tossed the sheathed weapon towards the middle of the room. The governor turned to the centurion and said, "Please resume and leave out no detail. I am especially interested to find out how our legate from Rome fathered a helio...helio...whatever in Britannia!"

Versillius responded, "It is a minor, but important detail and I will explain it shortly. Now, Appius Severus stated that his men were carrying out legitimate orders. But do the legate's instructions legitimately run to murder? You may not yet be aware of the circumstances, governor, but we have had two more murders this morning. We can add the deaths of Drusilla and the junior clerk Septimus, to the body count in our settlement. And as to the list of crimes we can also add two more. The theft of votive offerings from the temple and the attempted seizure of the contents of our fort's treasury."

"Don't listen to this fool, Quintus Lucius. Just get that big moron of his to move away from the door. Then I will personally travel to the west and summon the watch. I swear that they'll kill us all if you don't," the commanding officer replied.

The governor satisfied himself that both the legate and Trajanius were unarmed. He also checked that the only surviving bodyguard was securely bound, before he turned to Appius Severus and stating firmly, "For over ten years, you have treated me like a blithering idiot and made my life an absolute misery. I'm sick of your high handed attitude and patrician Roman ways. But they will not wash on this occasion. Now, Versillius has made some very serious accusations, which I have every intention of listening to. Please, continue with what you were saying, centurion!"

Surprised at the vehemence and resolve in the governor's tone, the legate put his head into his hands, as Versillius resumed, "Everything starts and ends with the audit, the census and Virulanium's wealth. There is no such exercise happening officially, on instructions from Eboracum or Londinium. We have no imperial writ in the township that I, or anybody else, have seen. All we have is just the legate's word for the audit. Antonius, being a meticulous scribe, was the first man to work that out, which was why the Appius Severus had him killed by his dupe Trajanius."

The skinny legionnaire swallowed heavily at this accusation. Again, Trajanius glanced at the legate, who in turn completely ignored him.

"On the night before the legate arrived here, Trajanius watched the scribe go to the house of pleasure. After he departed from there, Antonius was followed into the western forum. Where Trajanius murdered him in in cold blood. This was because he refused to give the legate unrestricted access to our treasury. Trajanius then stole his keys and robbed his office of the letters that had been delivered that day, because the communications from the legate might be considered incriminating."

"Why did he steal all the letters, including my note?" the governor asked.

"To confuse us and throw suspicion elsewhere," Versillius replied, before going onto say, "Trajanius was the legate's man on the inside of Virulanium. The murder of the chief scribe, on the day before the arrival of Appius Severus provided the legate with an ideal alibi."

The centurion paused for a moment, as Trajanius said, "It wasn't me...I didn't kill Antonius...I was on the night watch at the time. So I couldn't have done it, ask Marcus..."

" A watch that you were frequently absent from, as I recall," Marcus interjected.

"Partimius was the next to be murdered, as he had discovered some earlier correspondence from Deva. This also instructed the chief scribe to allow Appius Severus to carry out his audit and surrender the keys to the treasury. But even though the killer had seized Antonius' key ring, he didn't know one important fact. Only two people, the prefect and myself held the key to the treasury, on the town's master key ring. The junior scribe was killed beside the funeral pyre and the earlier communications seized."

As he paused briefly, to draw breath, the legate seemed to recover his composure and stated firmly, "This is all a pack of lies. I urge you again to restrain this man, governor, before this goes too far for your own good."

Quintus Lucius barely hesitated, before he replied, "Please resume, Versillius. Legate, as I said earlier, we really need to hear this man out. I'd be more than grateful, Appius Severus, if you would keep quiet, while he speaks."

The centurion then continued, saying to Quintus Lucius, "Both scribes were killed by a gladius. That should have told me that it was done by one of my soldiers, as we are the only garrison which still uses that weapon."

"What about the prefect and Juliana?" the governor asked.

"On the night of the feast, after you left in the company of Appius Severus, the prefect took me to one side. He told me that the legate had asked him for the keys to the treasury and unrestricted access. But he also said that he had refused the request, as there was no official documentation. That night we then had three more murders, so that the legate could obtain the prefect's keys to the treasury. And you might have had one more, if I didn't have my wits about me, when I returned to the barracks after the feast."

"But that was the Picts, who attacked you" the legate yelled at him, "You saw their blue body paint for yourself, man."

"Two days ago my men killed over twenty Picts, on your instructions," he replied, "While they were breaking their swords and spears, after the battle, I saw no body paint on their corpses. Only faded, blue tattoos which were etched deeply into their flesh. Marcus reminded me of that fact, after I was attacked. Of course any body can cover themselves in blue woad and darken their faces, can't they Vitellius?"

The captive nodded his agreement, and Versillius resumed, directing his words at the general, "Drusilla died in the morning, less than 12 hours after you fucked her in the prefect's vomitarium. That was so that the temple could be robbed of its votive offerings and other wealth. This would have been around the same time that I was being dismissed from service and Marcus was reduced to the ranks. Trajanius was the killer, because she died of a gladius wound." The legionnaire opened his mouth to protest, but thought better of it as Marcus picked up his baldric belt. He unsheathed the man's sword and held it up to the light. The governor shuddered at the sight of the naked blade. Although the sword had been cleaned there were still signs of visible, fresh bloodstains on it. Versillius shot him a glance of contempt and said, "Finally, as the only official left in the civic buildings, Septimus was killed so that the legate's bodyguard could rob the treasury. Which is where Marcus and myself found them, loading our settlement's assets into a cart, at the side of the building..."

The legate could sense that the argument was going against him and said, "If my men decide to behave in a criminal manner, then there is no way that I can be held to account for their behaviour. And the same applies to this renegade legionnaire, governor! I suggest that..."

"I'm not going to pick up the bill for this on my own," Vitellius shouted, "We were obeying your specific orders, as well you know."

Unable to answer the enlisted man, Appius Severus turned his face away. Trajanius decided to follow the other soldiers example and said, "Vitellius is right. We were all following his instructions...he is our leader!"

The centurion ignored him and continued, saying, "The reason for our legate's behaviour is simple, as I mentioned earlier; money. Marcus and I found a scrap of the missing correspondence in the junior clerk's hand, when we examined his body. There was only one legible word, solidus, our currency."

You're talking nonsense man," the legate interjected.

"I don't think so. You are about to return to Rome to follow the emperor Magnentius. It will take some means to live in the style that a man of your standing and ambition would require. If you rob Virulanium of its wealth and blame it on the Picts then your problem is solved. Add to that your pension and the favour of a new emperor and you would not have to work for another day in your life. You would want for nothing."

"I have to say, Appius Severus, that this is all fairly compelling," the governor stated, with a firmness in his voice that the centurion had never heard before.

"You know nothing, you old fool, if you are prepared to believe this disgraced man!" Appius Severus retorted back at him.

"It's all true," Vitellius interposed, "He had the four of us carry out the murders of the prefect and the robberies. We were promised that he would take us back to Rome and set us up in style."

"And no doubt he needed some soldiers to guard the stolen treasure, as he headed south," Versillius added.

"We were not going to head south," Vitellius said, "The legate has a fast ship waiting for us at *Arbeia*, on the east coast. That's why the garrison was sent westwards, along the wall. We'd have been away to the continent before the sun set."

The governor chortled to himself at these words and said, "But Versillius, you haven't explained this pater business to me yet. I'm still waiting to hear what that's all about."

"It's all to do with the cult of Mithras. Trajanius had attempted to revive the cult, because it made him feel important. But he was only the most important follower in Virulanium, a heliodromus. The legate is the cult's leader or pater. Although Trajanius tried to deflect my suspicions by claiming that the proconsul in Eboracum was their sponsor. There was another clue that I should have picked up on, when I was across the border..."

"You should have kept your mouth shut, like I instructed you to!" Appius Severus said to Trajanius.

"When I refused to burn the Pict's village," Versillius resumed, "Trajanius told me that it was the wish of our commanding officer to burn it. But I am his commanding officer, unless he was referring to the leadership of the cult!"
Versillius finished and having said all that he intended to say, fell silent.

For a few seconds nobody spoke, until the governor said, "Oh, dear me. What an awful mess, Appius Severus! Not that it gives me any great pleasure, but it seems that I am left with little alternative but to pass sentence you..."

The legate then seemed to recover some of his spirit and fight, saying, "You, pass sentence upon, me! How dare you even think about it? Stop this foolery now."

"I've thought about it and will do it. Now, for once you will shut up and listen. Unfortunately, as you mentioned in the late prefect's villa, to your great regret, we do not have punishment of crucifixion any longer. So I suppose you will have to be beheaded, along with our own legionnaire Trajanius. There is no way that seven murders can be allowed to go without retribution of the most severe kind. And I am sure that Virulanium's centurion will be more than capable and willing to carry out this most unpleasant job!"

"You are a just a native born Briton and cannot presume to sit in judgement on me!" the legate yelled, as Marcus moved towards him purposefully, "I was born in Rome of a high status family, which was helping to rule the empire while your ancestors were wallowing in mud and eating their own shit!"

"That maybe but I am the governor of the entire seventy three miles of Hadrian's Wall. This is a fact that you have totally ignored since my appointment ten years ago. I have not only the right, but also the full authority of Rome, to sit in judgement of you, Appius Severus. Now, Marcus and Versillius, take these two men out onto the parade ground and despatch them to the next world. While you are doing that, I will consider the fate of their remaining henchman."

"You can't execute me, centurion" Trajanius pleaded, "I beg you to show mercy. I was only carrying out the legate's orders..."

"You showed no mercy to Antonius, Partimius or Drusilla," Versillius told him, as he walked towards the man. Although the legate struggled and shouted, Marcus bound his arms firmly and easily manhandled him out of the barracks. Versillius did the same to Trajanius, who continued to plead for his life. Realising that his situation was hopeless the general stopped his resistance and yelling, when they emerged into the daylight. Versillius had taken up a large bladed spatha from the guardroom, as he could deliver a harder and cleaner blow with the longer weapon. This would make the execution less painful and swifter than using the centurion's shorter gladius. Out on the parade ground, the Marcus made Appius Severus kneel on the ground, which the legate did with some dignity. He then grabbed hold of Trajanius, who by now, was sobbing like an infant. Using the tip of the long sword, Versillius prodded the legate in the buttocks, making him flinch and extend his neck. The centurion then said, "Make your peace with whatever gods you believe in, Appius Severus."

There was no reply from the condemned man. After allowing him a few seconds, Versillius raised the long blade above his shoulders. Then, with one ferocious blow he removed the man's head from his body. As Trajanius saw the pater's head fall to the ground and the blood spurt from his neck, he fainted. It took Marcus some time to shake him awake and force him to kneel down. His tears were rolling down his cheeks, as he tried to steady himself. When Versillius prodded him and told the soldier to make his peace, he stuttered out the words, "Great Mithras, please save your obedient servant. Cautes and Cautophates, come to my..."

And then he spoke no more, as the spatha descended for a second time and severed the soldier's head from his body. The centurion told Marcus to wait until the legionnaires returned to the fort, before removing the dead men's remains from the parade ground. It would teach his century some good to see that nobody was above the severest punishments of the law. When they returned to his office, the governor looked at Vitellius and said to the two soldiers, "I've thought about an appropriate punishment for this man. It is my decision that he will suffer a most severe beating from the men of this garrison. In his case, I have decided to exercise leniency. You must agree that his testimony was quite useful, so try not to kill him. So I'd be grateful, Versillius, if you would organise that for me. Of course you are immediately reinstated in the army at your former rank, to serve out your last two months. But I also believe that our citizens owe you a great debt of thanks. If our money had been stolen, then I shudder to think of the consequences to our community. As the prefect used to keep telling me, it's not like we see any coffers from Rome arriving in Virulanium these days."

The two legionnaires took their captive out of the office. Marcus volunteered to await the return of the garrison, to arrange a punitive detail and administer the beating. Vitellius knew that he would suffer greatly, from the rods of his fellow soldiers. But he did feel relieved that unlike the legate or Trajanius, it seemed as if his head was going to remain on his shoulders.

Chapter Thirty Seven

The sun was starting to dip below the horizon, when the legionnaires from the garrison returned to the fort. They had spent a tiring and fruitless day looking for non-existent breaches in the Wall. Amid much grumbling, Versillius assembled them on the parade ground and explained the day's events. At this point, the moaning ceased, especially when they realised that the legate had been beheaded. Marcus then organised the beating of Vitellius, which left the legionnaire from Deva very bruised and extremely bloodied, but alive. The centurion did not participate in the punishment, as he had his own unfinished business to attend to, with Flavala. He removed his sword and went straight to the brothel, after leaving the barracks. She was more than pleased to hear about his reinstatement in the army and the regaining of his pension rights. After they had finally been able to make love, without any interruptions from Marcus, she said, "When you do retire, I've already decided that it will be time for me to sell the house of pleasure. We'll be able to live in your villa and invest the proceeds from the sale in a farm. That way there will always be a roof over our heads and enough food for us to eat and sell. How does that sound to you?"

Versillius sighed contentedly and replied, "It sounds fine to me. I'm getting far too old to be an attendant in your house of pleasure..."

"It's our brothel, soldier! From now on, we share everything, good and bad," she cut in, as her hand reached between his legs and she started to massage his penis, saying, "And don't think for one moment that you have completed our unfinished business. That was just the first instalment of your debt to me.

If you want our relationship to work well, Versillius, then you must realise that once is not going to be enough to satisfy my needs!" Knowing that he had met his match, the centurion lay back and let Flavala have her wicked way with him.

The next few days were quite traumatic for the small community of Virulanium. A lot of goodbyes and farewells had to be made. First it was the turn of Septimus, whose parents were inconsolable with grief, as he was their only son. In keeping with their Christian beliefs, he was interred with Brother Paulus presiding. Then the funeral pyres for Gaius Flavius, Juliana and their slave burnt long into the night. But apart from Quintillus, the acolyte, there were few people present to mourn the cremation of Drusilla. After the cremations were completed, the ashes were gathered up into clay urns and buried with ritual objects and offerings. The governor insisted that a detachment from Deva was sent to remove the bodies of the three dead legionnaires and the legate. Nobody in the vicus had any interest in their safe progression to the under world. But out of a sense of duty, Versillius arranged for the cremation of Trajanius. The centurion couldn't get away from the feeling that the legate had used the executed man. His instinct told him that Appius Severus had worshipped nobody but himself. And Trajanius would have been the ideal recipient for his ideas about Mithras. A dissatisfied and discontented legionnaire, suddenly offered importance and advancement...

The governor, who had now taken charge of all matters, military and civilian, also proved to be quite forgetful. But as Versillius noticed, this was only when it suited him. Quintus Lucius failed to remember that the temple's votive offerings and donations should have been returned to the religious institution. Instead he kept them in the town's treasury, where they had been left by Versillius and Marcus. In the absence of a high priestess there was nobody senior enough to object to this sad lapse of memory. Most of the soldiers were quite pleased with his "forgetfulness", because the issue of their withheld back pay was resolved overnight. Whenever Quintillus approached him on the topic of the temple's assets, the governor also seemed to suffer from sudden bouts of deafness. He was unable to hear a single word that the young acolyte was saying to him and sent him on his way. Quintus Lucius also took charge of the surviving member of the conspiracy to strip Virulanium of its wealth. Rather than send Vitellius back to Deva, to face imprisonment or penal slavery, he had the soldier dismissed from the army and imprisoned in Virulanium. Then he purchased the man from the civic administration, effectively making him a domestic slave. In fact, he became the governor's personal bodyguard. The former legionnaire came out of his complicity in the crimes, far better than any soldier could have expected to. Versillius always swore that Quintus Lucius was forever in Vitellius' debt, by having given him the means to dispose of the legate.

    A priestess, specially despatched from *Vindolanda,* married the centurion and Flavala within the month. Unsurprisingly, she also failed to make any headway with Quintus Lucius on the subject of the temple's assets. The couple had a traditional pagan wedding, which was conducted in the temple. The governor, the full complement of legionnaires and many citizens attended it. Even the centurion's trader friends from the lavatorium were present. They had already forgiven Versillius for the way in which he had conducted the murder investigation, feeling relieved that the killings had finished. Paribius even managed to make a speech at the reception, which was held in the barracks, which made no references to his still tender buttocks or bodily functions of any kind. Accordingly, it was a short speech, which nobody found in the least bit amusing. Although the bride and groom were rather thankful for this display of unusual restraint on his part.

Before the nuptials, Flavala set up home for them in the centurion's retirement villa. That was after she had made it fit for human habitation. His actual retirement took some time to come through - almost a year. This was because that while the governor was waiting for a new commanding officer to be sent from Rome, the centurion was promoted to the rank of acting prefect. Marcus was given his old job and became the youngest centurion stationed on Hadrian's Wall. It also meant that when Versillius eventually left the army, it was on a much higher pension than his previous rank had entitled him to. During his period of high office, one of the first things that he did was to convince Quintus Lucius that Partimius' widow, Getilla, should be granted a civic pension. Given the now healthy state of the civic treasury the governor was happy to agree to this request, as the man had been killed for carrying out his official duties. In the interim, he had persuaded Paribius to stay the interest accruing on the loan for her thatched house, paying off the capital himself.

It was the following year when the new legate, Sextus Vitruvius, arrived at the northern outpost of the empire. Like the late emperor Hadrian, he had been born in Spain and had seen service throughout the Roman world. This pleased the governor greatly, as the man had a much less arrogant attitude than his predecessor. It also pleased the soldiers, who could sense that he was one of their own, having risen through the ranks to his high position. A practical man, he wanted to work with the civic administration, rather than against it. Under the new prefect, Titus Viridius, the principae was reformed and reorganised. Titus was a career civil servant, who had previously been based at *Cilurnum*.

Just before Versillius was finally allowed to hang up his gladius, Flavala was true to her word. She sold the house of pleasure, to a wealthy man from Banna. He was looking for an investment opportunity, in the relatively wealthy settlement of Virulanium. They then bought an arable farm on the south side of the eastern vicus, close to the river. With the arrival of Sextus Vitruvius in Virulanium, the centurion was able to devote his time to Flavala and their farm. The both decided that children were out of the question, but possibly because of this, they enjoyed a happy and stable relationship for the next thirty years. But only the first ten years of their marriage was spent in Virulanium. This was because by 360 AD, barbarian incursions over the Wall had started to increase dramatically. The retired centurion quickly realised that the northern border was no longer practically defensible. While there was still an opportunity to find a buyer, they sold their farm. The couple then headed south to *Corinium*, which was the most important town in the south west and still safe from barbarian incursions. Retirement from the army did not mean the end of his career, because wherever there is a community, a man of Versillius' talents soon found his skills in demand.

Postscript

As I mentioned in the preface, Rome formally abandoned the Britain in 410 AD. In the years following 350 AD, contact with the continent had gradually declined, as disputes and invasions threatened the western empire. If the legate, Appius Severus, had returned to Rome his career as a follower of Magnentius would have been brief. The usurper's attempt to legitimise his seizure of the western empire soon ended. He was defeated by Constantanius II, at Mursa (modern day Croatia) in 351 AD. He later committed suicide in Gaul in 353 AD. Over the next one hundred and twenty years, the empire experienced periods of stability to go with the times of trouble. Most of these threats came from what we now call Germany. But the eternal city eventually fell to the Ostrogoths in 476 AD, ending almost one thousand years of western hegemony.

But that was not really the end of the Roman Empire, only the western and less wealthy part. The city that Constantine the first had founded on the site of an ancient Greek settlement in 330 AD, lived on and bore his name: Constantinople. It not only survived, but also prospered and became the centre of the civilisation known as Byzantium. It was not until 1453 AD that the eastern capital of the empire fell to the repeated attacks of the Ottoman Turks. Bearing in mind, that the Romans had overthrown the supremacy of their Etruscan neighbours in the sixth century BC, it means that the empire lasted as a physical entity, in one form or another, for over two thousand years. Which is why some historians call the Roman Empire the greatest power that the world has ever seen.

As for Hadrian's Wall, it is still with us to this day, but not in the form that the legionnaires of 350 AD would recognise. Versillius had been quite accurate in his assessment of barbarian activity. In 367 AD the north of England came under severe attacks from a coalition of Picts, Irish and Scots. Although this invasion was repelled, it took a tremendous amount of resources to turn the tide. In the meantime, Saxon incursions were becoming more frequent. When the final soldiers were recalled to the continent, the native people were left to fend for themselves. Like many other parts of Britain, the settlements along the wall suffered a similar fate. Although there were no immediate catastrophes, some historians estimate that within a few generations the benefits of belonging to Rome were lost. People forgot how to speak Latin and also how to read or write. Medicine, engineering and central heating vanished, to be rediscovered many years later. Civilisation effectively ceased to exist. The communities still existed, but became insular and defensive. They reverted to being like the tribes that the Roman invasion had conquered, with each defending its own territory. The Wall and its history were also soon forgotten. By the seventh Century AD, the Venerable Bede, who lived in Jarrow, believed that it had been built in the fifth Century AD - after the Romans had left Britain.

Over many hundreds of years, the stones blocks of the Wall and forts crumbled, as did the villas and thatched houses that surrounded them. They were also robbed out, by people on both sides of the border, to build their houses and boundary walls. For 350 years, from 1250 AD onwards, the Reivers occupied surviving forts and outposts. They were notorious bands of robbers, murderers and rustlers, who lead a lawless existence on either side of the border. Subsequently the mystery of the Wall was not rediscovered until the seventeenth and eighteenth centuries. But it was not until the nineteenth century that serious academic research and archaeological studies were made. This did have a downside. It meant that the many of their earlier renovations were made in the image, not always correct, of what the Victorians imagined the structure to be like. But since its rediscovery, our fascination with the Wall has grown and grown. In 1987 it was designated as a UNESCO world heritage site and continues to attract visitors from Britain and around the world.

Finally, a word on the cult of Mithras. On Hadrian's Wall there are the remains of four temples or Mithraeum dedicated to the deity. The best example can be found at Carrawburgh, or Brocolitia. Two other are located at Housesteads and Rudchester. There is at least one academic, active today, who believes that the cult of Mithras could easily have become the established religion in England, rather than Christianity. My view, is that the initiation ceremony's beatings would have put a lot of would be followers off joining the religion.

Glossary

Amphora: A clay vessel, of various sizes, used to store and transport goods.
Arbeia: South Shields. A 2nd Century fort and supply base for Hadrian's Wall.
Baldric: Narrow leather belt, worn off the shoulder. Supported the *Gladius*.
Banna: Birdoswald, fort and settlement. Sited on the river Irthing's mouth.
Ballista: A wooden Roman siege machine or catapult.
Barbarian: A savage person unable to speak Latin, who baas like a sheep.
Basilica: Stone walled building. The central room is taller than the side aisles.
Britannia: Britain, one of Forty Four Provinces of the Roman Empire.
Brocolitia: Carrawburgh. Site of the Wall's most complete Mithraeum.
Calderium: The hot room within a Roman bath.
Caligae: Military hob nailed, leather boots. (*)
Cautes: Attendant to Mithras. Represents sunrise.
Cautophates: Attendant to Mithras. Represents sunset.
Century: Roman army unit of EIGHTY man, not one hundred.
Cilurnum: Chesters, fort and settlement, located on the Wall.
Cingulum: Military leather belt, which had a protective groin sporran at front.
Civitas: A feeling of pride in performing one's civic duties.
Cognomen: A personal name or nickname. Distinguished family members.

Cohort: A unit of 480 men or six *centuries.*
Corax: Raven. In the cult of Mithras the first and lowest level of novitiate.
Corinium: Cirencester. The Most important settlement in the South West.
Dacia: Modern day Romania.
Denarius: A small silver coin. Also known as the 'double denarius'.
Deva: Chester, important fort and settlement. The base of Legion XX.
Eboracum: York, important fort and settlement. Historical base of Legion VI.
Frigidaria: Cold pool in a Roman bath house.
Germania: Germany
Gladius: Short Roman stabbing sword.
Greaves: Shin armour, worn by centurions. From the French word for shin.
Heliodromus: Runner of the sun. In the cult of Mithras sixth grade of novitiate.
Hypocaust: Roman under floor and wall heating system.
Intaglio: Seal of carved, oval glass, usually set in a silver ring.
Lavatorium: Public or private lavatory. Accommodated more than one person.
Legate: Commander of a legion, a general.
Leo: Lion. In the cult of Mithras the fourth level of novitiate.
Luguvalium: Carlisle, a westerly fort and settlement on the Wall.
Londinium: London, one of the most important Roman settlements in Britain.
Maile: Chain ring, linked upper body armour. A mail shirt.
Mithraeum: Dark, underground temple for the worship of Mithras.

Nomen: A family name, normally ending in -ius.
Palla or Pallium: Civilian Female or Male large, rectangular woollen cloak.
Paenula: Oval cloak, worn by legionnaires.
Pater: Father. In the cult of Mithras the seventh and highest grade of novitiate.
Patrician: Member of a family able to trace ancestry back to the Republic.
Perses: Persian. In the cult of Mithras the fifth level of novitiate.
Pilum: A javelin. Either heavy or light. The plural is *Pila*.
Praenomen: Name derived from father. Could denote patrician descent.
Principae: The headquarters or central administration buildings of a fort.
Pugio: A Roman dagger.
Scutum: A shield. Legionnaires used the oval shape from 3rd Century AD.
Segedunum: Wallsend, most easterly fort and settlement of Hadrian's Wall.
Segmentata: Plated metal armour. Believed to be the correct term.
Solidus: Coins of pure gold and silver which were not debased.
Spatha: A long bladed Roman sword which was also used by barbarians.
Subarmalis: Protective leather garment worn underneath armour.
Subligaculum: Linen underpants or loin cloth.
Tepiderium: Medium hot room in a Roman bath house.
Tessarae: Tiny cubes of stone, square or rectangular, used in a mosaic floor.
Tunica: Wool or woven linen garment.
Vallum: A southern ditch, which protected the rear of a settlement.

Valeria Victrix: Victorious Eagle. The Twentieth legion's title or nickname.

Vicus: Civilian settlement located on either side of a fort. The plural is *Vicii*

Vindolanda: Fort and settlement, south of Hadrian's Wall. Predates the Wall.

Vomitarium: A room set aside for the disgorging of food.

(*)

Caligae: The emperor Caligula derived his name from this article of footwear. The Roman army gave this to him, after his father Tiberius presented him to the soldiers, when he was a young boy. He was wearing a child's military outfit and the soldiers were taken by his tiny boots. They christened him Caligula, which means, "little boots".

I can be contacted at ktwc999@gmail.com, should any reader wish to comment on this novel.

Printed in Great Britain
by Amazon.co.uk, Ltd.,
Marston Gate.